Thumbprint Mysteries

HIT THE STREET

BY

JUDITH ANDREWS GREEN

CB

CONTEMPORARY BOOKS

a division of NTC/CONTEMPORARY PUBLISHING GROUP
Lincolnwood, Illinois USA

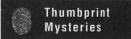
Thumbprint
Mysteries

MORE THUMBPRINT MYSTERIES

by Judith Andrews Green:

Without a Trace
Not a Chance

Dedication:
To Henrik

This is a work of fiction. The characters, incidents, and dialogues are products of the author's imagination and are not to be construed as real. Any resemblance to actual events or persons, living or dead, is entirely coincidental.

Cover Design: Alan Janson

ISBN: 0-8092-0680-3

Published by Contemporary Books,
a division of NTC/Contemporary Publishing Group, Inc.,
4255 West Touhy Avenue,
Lincolnwood (Chicago), Illinois 60646-1975 U.S.A.
© 1998 Judith Andrews Green
Manufactured in the United States of America.

890 QB 0 9 8 7 6 5 4 3 2 1

CHAPTER 1

"You're going to get yourself killed! Why can't you have a normal job?"

Justin Cobb stared into his coffee cup and let his girlfriend's words roll right over him. They had this argument almost every day, it seemed, and he was getting tired of it.

She didn't like his job—but after all, it was his job. He liked it just fine. He didn't make much money as a bicycle messenger, but that didn't bother him. He enjoyed the freedom of zipping around the city all day, on his own, with no one to bother him. He enjoyed beating the traffic. He could always find a way to squeeze his bicycle through a line of cars. He always got the package to where it was going. More than anything, he loved racing down the city streets, legs pumping, feeling the wind in his face. More than anything, he loved speed.

This time it was his own fault. He should have kept his mouth shut! Why did he have to go and tell Heather about the near miss that he'd had this afternoon? Someone had opened the door of a parked car just as he came whipping by. He'd had to swerve out in front of a truck that was coming the other way. It had been a close one, but he'd gotten through it all right. So why on earth did Heather have to get so upset?

"One of these days you're going to get run over, and that will be that!" Heather was saying. "You'll never even know what hit you!"

"I know how to look out for myself," Justin said. He stood up and tucked his helmet under his arm. "Well, thanks for the coffee. I'd better get going. I have to pick up one more package downtown. They wanted me there right at 4:00." He looked at his wristwatch. "Yikes! I'd better hurry! I've only got ten minutes!" He grinned at her. "Don't worry, I'll be careful. See you later!" He jammed the helmet on his head, grabbed his neon yellow jacket, and ran out the door into the hall, slamming the door behind him.

Heather walked over to the window and watched him push his bicycle down the front steps of her apartment building. He had to dodge around her landlady, fat old Mrs. Grasso. She was waddling up the front steps carrying her nasty little poodle. The poodle started yapping loudly, blocking out Mrs. Grasso's words as she called after Justin. Heather could just imagine what she had to say.

Justin never looked back. He jumped onto the bicycle, bumped off the curb, and cut in front of an oncoming car. The driver of the car slammed on the brakes and leaned on his horn. Justin just waved. Then he crouched down over his handlebars and sped off down the street. The last thing Heather saw of him was a flash of his yellow uniform as he pulled out around a black panel truck.

She shook her head. That Justin! He always waited until the last moment. Then he had an excuse to speed and take chances. Sighing, she turned away from the window and began to clear away the coffee cups.

*　　*　　*

At 4:02 Justin had picked up his last package for the day. By 4:25 he had delivered it to an office on the sixth floor of a big new building downtown. It was quitting time. As he walked to the elevator, he thought about the evening ahead of him. He'd been planning to spend it with Heather. After their argument this afternoon, he wasn't sure he wanted to see her again right away. Maybe he'd just go home and see what was on television.

Suddenly he heard a voice behind him. "Hey, you!"

Justin turned. A tall, well-built man in his forties was walking toward him down the hall. The man was wearing an expensive, dark gray suit. Somehow he didn't look like the other businessmen that Justin dealt with every day. There was a hard, alert look in the man's eyes, and the body under the expensive suit was ready for action. *This guy doesn't just sit behind a desk all day*, Justin thought. *Maybe he plays a lot of sports.*

"You want me?" Justin asked him.

"Yes, you. What's your name?"

"Justin, sir. Justin Cobb."

"You work for one of those bicycle delivery companies, right? Can you deliver a package for me? Now?"

"Well, sir, it's kind of late in the day. I was headed home. I really wouldn't have time to check it in before the office closes—"

"Fine. Then it's just between you and me. Here's the package, and here's your payment in advance. I think you'll find it's plenty." The man thrust a small, square package and a thin white envelope at him. The package had a name printed on it—Albert Worth—and an address on South 13th Street. The envelope was blank.

"The envelope's for you, Justin Cobb." The man was looking at Justin as if he were memorizing him. "I want that package at that address just as fast as you can get it there. Give it to no one else but Mr. Worth. Can I trust you on this?"

"Yes, sir," Justin stammered. The man nodded once, then turned and walked down the hall. In a moment, he had disappeared around the corner.

Only then did Justin look into the white envelope. All it had in it was one slip of green paper: a $500 bill.

Justin whistled softly to himself. He was used to getting tips, but he'd never had a tip this big! He could take Heather out to a really nice restaurant for dinner, to show her that he could really make something of himself with this job. He'd still have enough money left over to fix his racing bike and get it back on the road. This day was turning out better than he'd thought!

He stuck the package into his delivery pouch and punched the button for the elevator. For a tip like this, he'd make sure the man got extra fast service! In a moment, he was on his bicycle and out in the stream of cars and trucks pushing their way though the city streets.

Traffic was hung up on South Third Street with a big truck double-parked in front of a store. *What a time of day to be making a delivery*, Justin thought. He cut between two parked cars. Then he yanked on the handlebars and jumped his bicycle up onto the sidewalk.

He zipped around two old ladies with shopping bags. He cut in front of the deliveryman as he unloaded a big box. Soon he was back out on the street before anyone could even yell at him.

He grinned to himself as his bicycle whirred smoothly on down the street. He was making great time. Boy, was he good!

Then his luck ran out.

He was coming up to the corner of South Third Street and Randall Avenue. He timed it to hit the intersection just as the light turned green, so he'd be the first one through. He was keeping an eye on a small red delivery truck that was waiting at the corner, in case the driver jumped the light.

He never saw the taxi speeding up Randall Avenue.

The taxi driver was watching the red truck too. When the truck didn't move right away as the light changed, the taxi driver decided to rush on through. Just then Justin darted into the intersection.

With a squeal of tires—and a blast on the horn—the taxi slammed on the brakes. Justin swerved out of the way. He felt a gust of wind as the taxi passed him. It was so close that he could feel the heat of the engine and smell the burned rubber of the tires. The horn roared in his ears like a passing train. Then the taxi was past him and gone.

Horns blared all around him. What else was coming? Which way should he dodge? He tried to straighten himself out, but he had cut the bicycle so sharply that he was tipping over. The city street whirled around him— He was falling—

At that instant, the little red truck pulled into the intersection. The driver of the truck saw him but too late.

He jammed on the brakes so hard that the truck went into a skid, sliding, sliding toward Justin. As Justin leapt away from the screeching tires, the fender clipped his elbow hard, and he went down. The pavement rushed up at him and knocked the wind out of him with a whoosh. Behind him, there was a scrunch of metal.

He lay for moment with his face on the pavement, gasping, trying to draw a breath. All around him, car horns blatted and blared like angry bees. He felt sick and dizzy, desperate for air. The pavement was gritty and smelled of oil, but at least it wasn't moving.

"Are you okay?" a man's voice was asking.

His bicycle! That scrunch of metal must have been his bicycle! With a huge effort, Justin pulled some air into his aching lungs. Then he dragged himself to his feet and turned around.

His delivery bicycle was sticking out from under the truck at a strange angle. The twisted mess of metal that used to be the front wheel was crushed under the truck's front tire.

"Hey, man, are you okay?" the truck driver asked again. Then, seeing that Justin didn't seem to be hurt, he did what people do when they get over being scared. He got mad. "What are you, some kind of idiot?" he shouted over the racket of car horns. He looked at Justin's yellow uniform, now ripped and dirty from his meeting with the pavement. "You're one of those bicycle delivery guys, right? You guys are all crazy! They shouldn't allow you out on the street!"

"All right, all right. What's the matter here?" asked a heavy voice. A policeman was picking his way toward them through the tangle of cars and trucks in the intersection. The policeman looked at Justin's bicycle sticking out from under the truck. He looked at Justin's uniform and the pouch which hung by one strap from his neck. Justin guessed by the look on his face that his opinion of bicycle messengers was the same as the truck driver's.

And he was right. The policeman looked Justin in the eye, as if he were daring him to complain. "Well, son," he said, "it looks like you'll have to come down to the police station."

*   *   *

It was hours later when Justin finally left the police station. It was certainly too late for a fancy dinner with Heather. He didn't really want to face her right now anyway. She'd want to know about the scratches on his face. That would set her off again about his job.

Of course, he wasn't sure how much longer he'd have the job. The boss hadn't been happy when he had called from the police station. He was on probation until further notice. And if the boss ever found out about the package he'd picked up this afternoon! Well, that would be the end of it.

He didn't think anyone would still be at the address on South 13th Street, but he had to give it a try. He had to get rid of the package before the boss caught him with it. Or the guy in the business suit who'd given him that fat tip.

It was beginning to get dark as he got off the bus at the corner of South 13th and Howard. He walked down 13th Street, reading the numbers on the fronts of the buildings as he passed. The street was quiet. On a Friday night, people really cleared out of these office buildings.

Up the block, a movement caught his eye. A man had come out of a building and was hurrying down the steps. In a moment the man had snapped open the door of a car parked at the curb and jumped in. The car door slammed shut and the engine revved at almost the same instant. "Someone's in a hurry," Justin said to himself.

The car pulled away from the curb as Justin came toward it—a shiny new black Jaguar, low and slinky. The engine gave a deep roar of power as the car shot through the gears and sped away. "Nice wheels!" Justin muttered. "Sweet!"

He stopped for a moment to watch the Jag make the corner at full speed and disappear. Then he went on looking at the building numbers.

Number 2344 was the building that the driver of the car had come from. This was the place. Maybe someone was still there after all. Or had Justin missed him?

It was a big office building, fifteen or twenty stories high, new, with lots of glass. Justin trotted up the front steps and through the wide glass front door. He nodded to the guard at the front desk, hoping the guy wouldn't notice the dirt on his uniform. Then he headed for the elevator.

The office he wanted was on the sixth floor. The small wooden sign on the door said simply PUBLIC WORKS. The door was locked.

Justin knocked loudly and put his head close to the door to listen. There was no sound, no one moving about inside. "Mr. Worth?" Justin called. He looked again at the name on the package: Albert Worth. "Mr. Worth, package for you!"

No one answered. Justin shrugged. He'd have to try again first thing on Monday. He shoved the package back into his pouch. Then he headed for home and a hot shower.

*   *   *

Justin slept late on Saturday morning. He woke up a bit stiff from his trip to the pavement the day before. *I ought to call Heather,* he thought. But his stomach was growling. Later. He'd call her later. He had to eat, didn't he?

He threw on some clothes and strolled down to the corner restaurant for coffee and a pile of fresh donuts. As he settled himself onto a stool, he picked up a newspaper from the counter. He skipped the front page with its big headline that said CITY OFFICIAL MURDERED. What he wanted was the sports section.

When his food came, he stirred a heaping spoonful of sugar into his coffee. He bit into the first donut before he went back to the newspaper. He glanced at the front page. *Albert Worth, 52,* it said, *a highly placed official in the Department of Public Works, was found dead in his office last night. When his wife reported that he had not come home for supper, police searched the office on South 13th Street and found—*

Justin felt the last bit of donut stick in his throat. South 13th Street? Public Works? This was beginning to sound like somewhere he'd been before! His eyes snapped again to the top of the article. *Albert Worth, 52, a highly placed official—*

Justin swallowed hard. The donut wouldn't go down.

"Hi, Justin," said a familiar voice behind him. "I was looking for you. I sort of expected you'd come over last night."

Justin spun slowly around on his stool. As he turned, he let his elbow push the newspaper onto the floor behind the counter. "Hello, Heather," he said. "What's up?"

CHAPTER 2

After Heather came into the coffee shop, Justin gave up even trying to eat his breakfast. He left the donuts on the counter and walked Heather back to her apartment.

She was chattering away, talking about this and that. He didn't hear any of it. Anytime she slowed down, he just said, "Mmm," and she started talking again.

They were walking past a newsstand with newspapers and magazines stacked up all around it. Justin could see the big black headline over and over: CITY OFFICIAL MURDERED. "Look over there!" he told Heather, pointing across the street.

"What? What do you see?" Heather asked, looking all around.

Justin dragged her past the newsstand. "There was a cute little kitten in front of that building," he said quickly. "Didn't you see it? It must have gone down the alley."

Heather stopped in the middle of the sidewalk. "We just passed the newsstand," she said. "Don't you want to stop and get a paper? I can't believe you aren't jumping at a chance to read the sports section!"

"No! No, I, um, watched the game on TV last night. Let's go!" Justin yanked on her arm.

"Justin, is something wrong?" Heather asked. "You're being so quiet! Is everything all right?"

"Everything's fine!" Justin said as he walked on down the street, pulling her with him. But he could feel the newspapers behind him, pile after pile of them, with their big black headlines about Albert Worth.

Mrs. Grasso was sitting on the front steps of Heather's building, enjoying the sunshine. Her little dog was sniffing around a bit of grass in front of the building, but then it saw Justin coming up the sidewalk. The dog ran at him, barking and yapping and snapping its tiny jaws.

"Hey, Fifi! What do you think you are, a big mean watchdog?" Mrs. Grasso was laughing so hard that her eyes disappeared above her fat, pink cheeks. "Are you going to protect me from that Mr. Cobb? I don't think we need to worry about Mr. Cobb knocking us over today. He hasn't got his yellow uniform on." She put her head to one side and fluttered her eyelashes at Justin. "We think Mr. Cobb looks very handsome when he's not wearing his yellow uniform, don't we, Fifi?"

Fifi didn't seem to care whether Justin was wearing his uniform or not. The little dog went right on yapping at Justin and trying to bite at his running shoes. The dog finally grabbed one of Justin's shoelaces in its teeth and pulled, growling. Mrs. Grasso just laughed and laughed, jiggling up and down on the step, gasping for breath.

Justin tried to get free. The dog wouldn't let go until Heather bent down and gently took the shoelace out of its teeth. Then it ran back to Mrs. Grasso and jumped up into her lap.

"Well, Heather," Mrs. Grasso said, wiping her eyes with the back of her hand, "what are you young people up to this beautiful morning? Are you making any big plans today?" And she gave Heather a huge wink.

Heather's face turned bright red. "No, um, not much, Mrs. Grasso," she stammered. "It *is* a beautiful day, isn't it?"

"So did you see the newspaper this morning?" Mrs. Grasso asked. "Some city official downtown got murdered!"

Justin felt his heart drop into his running shoes. "Oh, that's too bad," Heather was saying loudly, as if she was glad to change the subject away from her future plans. "Did you hear about that, Justin?"

Quickly, before she could see his face, Justin bent down to tie his shoelace. "Um, no, I don't think so," he mumbled.

"I don't know what this city is coming to!" Mrs. Grasso said. "It's getting so that it's not safe anywhere!"

"Yeah, well, I think I have to get going," Justin said. "I have some things I have to do." He stood up, keeping his face turned toward the street, away from Heather. "I'll call you, Heather. Maybe this afternoon. Good-bye, Mrs. Grasso, nice to see you."

He took off down the sidewalk, walking fast. Behind him, he heard Mrs. Grasso say, "Such a lovely young man!"

Just then the dog started barking again, so he couldn't hear what Heather answered. He wasn't sure he wanted to know.

Justin couldn't think about anything except Albert Worth and the package. He kept thinking of himself standing there in the hall of the office building on South 13th Street, knocking on Albert Worth's office door, calling his name. And all that time, Worth was lying on the floor in there—dead.

Who *was* Albert Worth? What happened to him? Why was he murdered? Did the package have anything to do with it?

If he hadn't had that accident on the way to deliver the package—If he had gotten there sooner—Would Albert Worth still be alive?

The man who was hurrying down the front steps when Justin got to the building—was that the killer? *No!* Justin told himself. The building on South 13th Street was a big one with lots of offices. The man in the black Jaguar could have come from any one of them.

The package couldn't have anything to do with Albert Worth's death, he told himself. It was just bad luck, that's all. Just bad luck.

Please let it be just bad luck!

*   *   *

When Justin got back to his apartment, he closed the door and locked it. He threw the second bolt too, the one that he almost never used. There, that felt better.

Then he turned around and saw his pouch lying on the couch where he had dropped it the night before. The delivery pouch with Albert Worth's package still in it.

What if Heather came over? She might pick up the pouch and see the package! He dashed across the room, grabbed the pouch, and looked around wildly for someplace to hide it.

If only it were Monday, he could get rid of the package! But what was he going to do with it on Monday? Take it to the Public Works office and ask for Mr. Worth? And what if Heather saw him on his way there? She would be heading for her job at the day care center, and she might see him. Justin's mind was racing with one worry after another. What was he going to do?

There was a knock on the door. Justin just stood there in the middle of the floor and stared at the door. He couldn't move. Another knock. Then a voice saying, "Hey, Justin, you in there?"

"Who—Who is it?" Justin called out.

"It's me!" the voice said.

"Hugo? Is that you?"

"Yes, it's me, Hugo! Who do you think it is, the Queen of England? Come on, man, open the door!"

Feeling as if he were waking up from a dream, Justin went to the door. He unlocked the bolts and opened the door for Hugo, his neighbor from upstairs. Hugo slouched in, wearing an old green sweatshirt with a huge hole under one arm, blue jeans, and pink bedroom slippers. "What's going on, man?" he asked. "You've got this place locked up tighter than the bank!"

"Oh, well, I—" Justin stammered.

"I came to borrow your can opener," Hugo said. "I know I've got one up there somewhere, but I can't seem to find it. I think I had it yesterday, but it's gone now. I can't have breakfast without a can opener. There isn't anything to eat in my kitchen that hasn't gone bad except for a can of beef stew."

"My can opener?" Justin said, still in a daze. "Sure. Just a moment." He started to head for the corner of the apartment that served as his kitchen. Then he stopped and turned around. "Hey, wait a second. That *was* my can opener! You borrowed it on Thursday!"

"It was?" Hugo shrugged. "Well, don't get into a tizzy. It's up there somewhere. I've just got to think about it, that's all." He followed Justin across the room and looked past him at his refrigerator. "Well, if you don't have another can opener, what have you got to eat?"

Justin yanked open the cupboard door and pulled out a box of dry cereal. "Here!"

"Thanks!" Hugo said. "This is my favorite kind! How about some milk? And do you have a clean bowl?"

Justin waved toward the cupboards. "Anything you want," he said tiredly. "Go for it."

Hugo took a bowl and filled it to the brim with cereal. He then poured the milk in too fast, so that some of the cereal spilled onto the floor. While he was digging in the drawer for a spoon, he ground the spilled cereal into the floor under his feet. "So what are you up to?" he asked with his mouth full of cereal. "Are you off to make a delivery?"

Justin realized that he was still holding the pouch under one arm. He set it down quickly on the table. "No," he said. "I was just putting it away. It's from yesterday."

Hugo nodded and shoved another huge spoonful of cereal into his mouth. "Right. It's Saturday, isn't it?" he said. "Hey, I'm a working stiff now too! I'm starting a new job downtown on Monday. I'm going to work on the computers for the City Housing Department in one of those fancy new buildings down on South 13th Street!"

Justin jumped. "South 13th Street!" he gasped. Couldn't he ever get away from that address?

Then he had an idea. "Hey, I have one package left over from yesterday that I didn't have a chance to deliver

before the office closed. It's for a place on South 13th
Street. Do you think you could take it over on Monday
morning and just drop it off? If I have to go way over
there, I'll be late for work. I'm already in trouble with
the boss because I had a little problem with my delivery
bicycle yesterday." Justin realized the words were coming
out faster and faster. He made himself slow down. "The
bicycle ended up under a truck. They're going to have to
give me a new bike on Monday. So if you could take the
package on your way to work—"

"Sure, man. No problem." Hugo pushed the rest of the
cereal into his mouth and filled the bowl again. He added
more milk, spilling more cereal onto the floor. Then he
held out one hand for the package.

Justin opened the delivery pouch and pulled out the
package. "The address is right on it," he said. "Just drop it
off with anyone at that office. I think it's Public Works."
As he handed Hugo the package, he watched his face to
see if he recognized the name from the newspaper
headlines. But Hugo wasn't thinking about anything
except pushing the cereal into his mouth. "Thanks a lot,"
he added.

"No problem," Hugo said again. He tucked the package
under his arm and headed for the door, carrying the bowl
with him. "Thanks for breakfast," he said and disappeared
out the door.

Justin breathed a sigh of relief. The package was gone.
There was just one more thing he had to take care of.

He found his uniform where he had thrown it over a
chair. He took the white envelope out of the pocket. He
stood holding it for a moment, looking all around the
room. Finally he took the $500 bill out of the envelope
and shoved it under the dirty clothes in the bottom of his

closet. He tore the envelope into little pieces and flushed them down the toilet.

Then he walked over to the window and stood looking out at the traffic moving up and down the street.

*   *   *

Justin took Heather to the movies on Saturday night. On Sunday they took a long walk to the park. Anything to get away from his apartment and the $500 bill that seemed to be burning its way through the dirty clothes at the bottom of his closet. Anything to get away from thinking about the package and Mr. Worth.

But it was hard to think about anything else. Just for something to talk about, Justin started telling Heather about Hugo and the can opener.

"How does that guy get from one day to the next?" Heather laughed. "What does he live on?"

"He has a new job," Justin told her. "Something about computers." He was careful not to tell her where—he didn't want to say anything about South 13th Street. "He starts on Monday."

"Oh, he'll probably forget to go. Someday he'll just forget to breathe, and that will be the end of him," Heather said.

"Well, um—" Justin felt crunched up inside. Why had he trusted Hugo with that package? Why did he think Hugo would ever remember it? "Let's go out to eat!" he said, just to change the subject. "Where would you like to go?"

*   *   *

The weekend seemed to go on forever, but at last Monday came, as it always does. Before he headed for work, Justin ran up the stairs to knock on Hugo's door.

Hugo was just coming out of his apartment. He was dressed for work in a shirt, jacket, and pants that weren't too wrinkled. He was even wearing regular shoes, and his long, shaggy hair was combed neatly. Justin hardly recognized him. He suddenly felt very foolish, standing there in his yellow uniform with the badly mended tear in the sleeve.

"I'm off to the world of work," Hugo said in a loud voice, as if he were speaking on television. "I'm off to save the City Housing Department from its big, bad computers."

"Um—Do you have that package?" Justin asked.

Hugo smiled and patted his jacket pocket. "It's right here. Don't worry about a thing. I'll drop it off on my way. See you later." Whistling, he went down the stairs.

As Justin watched him go, he felt better than he had since he first got the package on Friday afternoon. Everything would be all right now. It had to be.

*   *   *

Justin felt better right up to the moment he got to work.

"You'll find your new delivery bicycle in the back room," his boss snarled at him. "See if you can keep from busting this one up! I can't stay in business if I have to keep buying new bicycles for people who can't keep their eyes open! And what did you do to your uniform? Look at you! Do you think I want you running around the city looking like that, with my company's name written across your back? Get in the back room and pick yourself out a new shirt! And you'll find the price of it taken out of your next paycheck!"

Justin stamped into the back room with his boss's angry words still following him. His boss was just worried

about the bicycle and the uniform. He never asked if
Justin had been hurt. He knew darned well his delivery
people took chances so that they could make their
deliveries fast. He expected them to take chances! But if
anyone had a moment of bad luck—Justin pulled a new
yellow shirt off the rack and put it on. For two cents he'd
quit this job!

Then he saw the new bicycle. It was a beauty—sleek
and shiny, gleaming silver. He knew it would be fast.

In a moment he had picked up his first assignment,
and he was out on the street pedaling like crazy. The new
bike hummed under him as he sped along, zipping in and
out of the traffic. He whipped around the corner onto
Newell Street. He jumped up on the curb at the
intersection just for the fun of it and popped off between
two parked cars. Then he whizzed down Newell Street
without a care in the world.

He was having a great time trying out what the bicycle
would do. He was having such a good time that he never
noticed the black Jaguar pulling away from the curb as
he went by.

The Jaguar turned the corner onto Newell Street,
moving in and out of traffic to keep a steady two cars
behind him as he pedaled happily down the street.

CHAPTER 3

It was about noon when Justin first spotted the black Jaguar.

He had made five deliveries, and he was whizzing down North Sixth Street with two more packages in his pouch. Suddenly he glimpsed the black Jaguar in the tiny rearview mirror that was hooked onto his helmet. It made him jump when he saw it.

He had begun to forget about Albert Worth, the package, and everything else that had happened on Friday night. Seeing a black Jaguar brought it all back to him for a moment. He was glad that Hugo had taken care of the package for him that morning. He shook his head, glad that it was all over.

Then he shot around the corner onto Reese Street, cut between two motorcycles that were riding side by side, and made another right onto North Seventh

Street. He jumped the bicycle up onto the sidewalk and hopped off. As he dashed into an office building, he pulled one of the packages out of his pouch.

He had already forgotten about Friday night and black Jaguars. He didn't see this one go slowly by. He didn't see the driver watching him hurry through the big glass doors of the office building with a package in his hand.

*   *   *

That afternoon, he spotted the black Jaguar again, three cars behind him on Richmond Street. It gave him the creeps, but he wouldn't let himself worry. *There are lots of black Jaguars in the world,* he told himself. *There are probably dozens of Jaguars driving around this city.*

On Tuesday morning, he spotted it twice. He began to watch for it. *It wouldn't be hard for someone to see me,* he thought. *I go riding around in this crazy yellow suit with the company name across my back.*

He kept a lookout in his rearview mirror. There always seemed to be a black Jaguar back there somewhere. By quitting time on Tuesday, he was sure he was being followed.

He went home a different way than he usually went. He took some extra turns, doubling back a few times, and finally cut through an alley that was too narrow for a car. By the time he got home, he was quite sure no one could have followed him.

He locked the bicycle in the cellar of his building and climbed up the stairs, pulling off his helmet as he went. He dug in his pocket for his keys and unlocked his door.

He stood in the doorway with his mouth hanging open.

His apartment was a disaster. His bed had been pulled apart, and the mattress was upside down on the floor. Everything that had been in the kitchen cupboards had been dumped on the counter or on the floor. The clothes from his closet had been thrown everywhere. His bureau drawers hung open. His socks and underwear were heaped up, as if an animal had been burrowing in them. His television set was pulled around backwards, away from the wall. Every book from the bookcase had been yanked out, opened, and thrown down. His bicycle magazines had been opened and tossed helter-skelter onto the floor.

His bicycle! What had they done to his racing bicycle? He leapt into the room and whirled around to look at it. It stood against the wall, untouched. That was a relief!

But oh, the rest of it! He pushed the door shut and just stood and stared at the mess. He shut his eyes tight and then opened them again, but the mess was still there.

For crying out loud, he thought, *my apartment looks worse than Hugo's ever did!*

Then the phone began to ring.

It looked so normal, hanging there on the wall, ringing away as if everything around it was normal too. He made his way to it around the heaps of his belongings on the floor and picked up the receiver. "Hello?"

"Hi, Justin," said Heather's voice. "I just got out of work, and I thought I'd come over. Maybe I could fix us some supper. Okay?"

"No!" Justin squeaked. Then he added, "I can't see you tonight! I've got, um, too much work to do!"

"Too much work? Are you making deliveries at night now? Oh, Justin, that's even more dangerous than in the daytime!"

"No, no, I'm not making deliveries. No, I've got work to do around here. I've got to—Well, I've got to clean my apartment."

"I'll help you!" Heather said. "I don't mind at all. Really!"

"That's very nice of you, but I've got to do it myself. Thanks anyway. Look, I'll call you tomorrow, okay? Tomorrow. I promise. Good-bye."

As he hung up the phone, he could hear Heather's voice calling out, "But Justin—"

He leaned against the wall with his head in his hands. Things were going from bad to worse, and he didn't know what to do.

He was being followed, and someone had ransacked his apartment. Should he go to the police? What would he say to them? *I took five hundred bucks to deliver a package for some guy without telling my boss about it, but I didn't deliver it, and the guy I was supposed to give it to ended up dead.* Yeah, that would sound great.

He couldn't let Heather get involved. What if she got hurt? He couldn't let that happen. He'd already done enough damage!

He knew one thing, though. Heather was beginning to wonder what was going on. If his life didn't straighten itself out soon, he was going to lose her. And, he suddenly realized, he really didn't want that to happen.

He looked around the apartment again and felt his shoulders droop. Cleaning up this mess was going to take half the night.

With a sigh, he made his way to the heap of clothes and began hanging them up again in the closet. Except for the fact that his clean clothes were mixed in with the dirty clothes that had been on the floor of the closet, nothing was torn or broken. *This could have been a lot worse*, he thought. *Whoever did this was looking for something. They must have been looking for the package. If they'd gotten mad when they didn't find it, they could have busted everything.*

As he worked his way down the pile of clothes, he began to find tiny scraps of green paper. At first he didn't know what they were.

Then he figured it out. Whoever had ransacked his apartment did get mad at him. The green paper had been money. The scraps were shreds of the $500 bill.

As he worked, Justin listened for Hugo's footsteps on the stairs to his apartment. A couple of times he thought he might have heard someone. When he ran out into the hall, no one was there.

Hours went by. It was getting late. Hugo was always home by now, walking around up there, playing his stereo loud, maybe coming down to borrow something. Tonight there wasn't a sound from his apartment. Justin went up and pounded on his door, but no one came.

Bit by bit, Justin's apartment was beginning to look less like a disaster movie and more like someone lived there. The books were back in the bookcase. The clothes were back in the closet. The TV was facing into the room.

The kitchen took the longest, because some things had broken as they fell. There was broken glass, spilled cereal, and instant coffee to sweep up.

The searchers—somehow he knew there must have been at least two of them—had gone through his food, checking inside the wrappers. They had opened the ice cream in his freezer and taken the cap off the milk. He found a loaf of bread that had been squeezed until it was almost flat. He threw away most of his cereal and crackers, because he knew that the big gorillas had pawed through the boxes. He couldn't stand the thought of eating anything they might have touched.

All this time, there was no sign of Hugo.

Finally, around two o'clock in the morning, he put his bed back together and got into it. But he couldn't sleep. He lay awake listening. For what? Hugo? The big apes who had searched his apartment?

At last, just as it was beginning to get light outside, he fell into an exhausted sleep.

Soon afterward, the alarm clock went off. Justin snapped awake. For a moment, he wasn't sure what that noise was. What day was it? Why was he so *tired?*

Then he remembered everything: the package, the Jaguar, the trashing of his apartment.

He jumped out of bed, pulled on some clothes, and ran up the stairs to Hugo's apartment. He hoped to see Hugo just coming out of his door in his almost-neat outfit on his way to work. But the upstairs hall was empty.

He pounded on Hugo's door. No one came. There was no sound inside. All was quiet, just like the Public Works office had been last Friday night.

Shoulders drooping, Justin walked slowly back down the stairs to his apartment. He took a shower and made some hard-boiled eggs—at least he could be sure that no one had touched the insides of *them*. Then he pulled on his yellow uniform.

He felt like a target.

* * *

All morning he kept watch in his helmet rearview mirror for the black Jaguar. He didn't see it. Well, he didn't see it for sure. From time to time, he would catch a flash of shiny black in the tiny mirror. Then he would drive himself crazy trying to get a better look.

It wasn't the best way to be riding through city traffic. He had a number of close calls because he wasn't watching the drivers around him carefully enough. At one point he almost ran right into the back of a taxi that stopped suddenly to pick up a passenger. It was making him slower too. He wasn't diving for the openings in traffic the way he usually did. He made five deliveries before his lunch break. He probably could have made six or seven if he'd been really on top of things.

His boss wasn't happy. "So you finally got the package delivered to Randall Avenue, did you?" the boss snarled when he called the office for the next assignment. "How nice of you to call us! I hope we're not spoiling your peaceful morning by expecting you to do a little work as you ride around our fair city on your *brand new bicycle!*"

Justin didn't say anything. His boss was never happy, no matter how much work he and the other bicycle messengers did. He always thought they could move faster, think quicker, and squeeze more deliveries into a day's work. Justin just pulled out his notepad and asked for the next assignment.

It was for the head office of an airline at 3554 South 13th Street.

For a moment, Justin wanted to refuse the assignment. He wanted to tell the boss he wouldn't go, give it to someone else. He was never going near South 13th Street again.

Then he thought again. Hugo! This would give him an excuse to go see Hugo where he worked.

He rode down South 13th Street, looking at the signs on the buildings, watching for the City Housing Department. Suddenly he realized that he had gone right by number 3554. He had to backtrack and drop off his package. He called in from that address for his next assignment, which was three blocks over on South 16th Street. Now he had to really hurry if he was going to find Hugo's office.

Two blocks up, he found it. The City Housing Department took up a whole building in the 5000 block of South 13th Street. He jumped off the bicycle, dashed up the front steps, and rushed up to the front desk. "I have an important message to deliver!" he gasped.

The woman behind the desk looked up at him. "Who are you looking for?" she asked.

"The person's name is Hugo. He works in your computer department."

The woman began searching through a list of names and office numbers. "We don't really have a computer department," she said. "There are computers in every office. Let me see—I don't have a listing for a Mr. Hugo. Does that begin with an H?"

"He just started work yesterday," Justin explained. "And—um—Hugo is his first name."

The woman raised one eyebrow. "I see. And what is his last name?"

Justin swallowed hard. "I don't know his last name," he said. How could he explain that someone like Hugo didn't *need* a last name? "He's about my height, he's skinny, and he has long brown hair. He was wearing a light blue shirt and a green jacket, and his pants were kind of wrinkled—" He let his voice fade away. The woman was staring at him with both eyebrows raised.

"Over two thousand people work in this building," she said slowly and carefully, as if he weren't smart enough to understand her if she spoke quickly. "I'm afraid I can't think of anyone who quite matches that description."

Justin looked up the long hall that led away from the front door. There were doors all along the hall. There was a set of three elevators at the end, leading upward to more halls with more doors. Hugo could be behind any one of them. If Hugo was still alive.

"Would you like me to make a call to your messenger company?" the woman was asking. "It is clear that you need better directions."

Quickly, Justin turned so that she couldn't see the company name on his back. "No, thanks," he said. "I'll check back into the office myself." He backed up until he bumped into the front door and then slid out onto the street. Through the glass, he could see the woman behind the desk still watching him.

He wanted to hang around, to see if Hugo would come out for lunch. But the woman was looking at him so strangely that he figured he'd better move on. He got on his bicycle and headed for his next pickup on South 16th Street.

He spent the next few hours trying to keep his mind on his work. He made three deliveries in really good time which pleased him even if it wouldn't make his boss happy. For a while, he forgot about the black Jaguar and the tough-looking man in the business suit who had given him the package. *They've given up on me,* he told himself. *Everything will be all right now.*

At quarter to three, he was whizzing along the downtown section of Ash Street with a bulky package stuffed into his pouch when he came upon a big traffic jam. He worked his way up the line of cars that were crawling along Ash Street. He squeezed in next to the cars parked along the curb, dived into gaps in the traffic, and went up on the sidewalk when he had to. Then he came to the place where all the cars were headed.

It was a big church. People were flowing in, lots of people, well-dressed people. And right out front, a long black hearse stood waiting. Justin stopped next to a taxi that was letting off a passenger. "What's going on?" he asked the driver.

"It's a funeral for that official from Public Works," the driver said. "The one who was murdered last Friday."

CHAPTER 4

Justin couldn't make himself go on making deliveries that day.

When he dropped off the package that he was carrying, he called the office and told the boss he was going home sick. When the boss started yelling about his being on probation, he said he thought he was going to throw up and hung up the phone.

"Are you okay?" asked a woman who was standing nearby.

"Yeah, I'm fine," Justin said. But he wasn't. He was tired and sad and scared out of his mind.

He had to find Hugo! He had to get that package back! If the guy in the black Jaguar caught up with him, and he didn't have the package—

What was *in* the package, anyway? What could be so important that they would kill someone for it? It couldn't be money. The gorillas who searched his apartment didn't take the $500 bill—they just ripped it up to teach him a lesson. There must be plenty more where that came from.

He tried to remember what the package felt like. It was in a small brown packet. It wasn't heavy. It was flat—Maybe a computer disk.

Uh, oh. What if Hugo had opened the package? What if it *was* a computer disk, and Hugo stuck it into a computer somewhere, and—

Justin didn't know enough about computers to know what could happen next. Maybe all the computers in the city would break down at the same moment. Or the Pentagon would suddenly blow up in Washington, D.C. Something crazy like that.

Crazy. Yeah, that's me. This is driving me crazy, Justin thought. *I've got to get some rest before I go right around the bend.* He got on his bicycle and slowly pedaled home.

As he came around the corner on his own block, he was hardly watching where he was going. He was looking at the pavement just a few feet in front of him, deep in thought. A car horn blared in the distance. He glanced up to make sure he wasn't going to run into something.

Out of the corner of his eye, he caught a flash of shiny black metal just turning the next corner beyond the front of his apartment building. His heart froze inside his chest. The Jaguar! Going around the block for another try! Circling, circling, waiting for him!

With a strangled cry, he shot across the intersection and down the opposite street. He dove into the first alley he came to. He pedaled like mad down the alley and yanked the bicycle around behind a big dumpster. He shoved the bicycle between the dumpster and the wall behind it. Then he scrunched himself down into the corner behind some garbage bags and waited.

He could hear his heart hammering, as if it were going to break right out of his chest. His breath rasped in and out of his throat like a file dragging across a block of wood. His hands were shaking, and his knees felt like jelly.

Bit by bit, his heart slowed down to normal. His breathing quieted. He stopped shaking. He began to notice the smell of the garbage bags around him. The one next to his head was extra bad, probably full of rotten fish cuttings or something from the restaurant near the corner. Something was poking into his back where he was crouched up against the dumpster.

What was he doing here, anyway? He counted to one thousand, just to give himself some more time, in case the driver of the black Jaguar had seen him pedal into the alley. No one came. There was no sound of footsteps, no voices. Just the normal sounds of traffic on the street.

He stood up and looked around. He couldn't stay here in the alley, that was for sure. Now that he wasn't so scared, he felt as if the smell from the dumpster was going to knock him over. But where could he go?

He couldn't go back to his apartment. It would only be a matter of time before the big apes who had searched his apartment decided to search *him*. They might decide to take him apart the way they'd taken apart his kitchen. Or Albert Worth.

He thought for a moment of heading out of the city. He could go stay with his mother. But he rejected that idea almost as soon as he'd thought of it. For one thing, his mother would fuss and fret and want to call the police. She'd never been the same ever since his father had taken off eight or ten years ago. He didn't want to give her anything new to worry about. For another thing, his wallet was still at his apartment in his pants pocket, hanging on the chair next to his bed. All he had in the pocket of his uniform was a dollar and a small amount of loose change.

He looked down at the uniform. The yellow color could be seen three or four blocks away. That was why the delivery company made the messengers wear it. But it sure wasn't helping him now.

He pulled off the yellow shirt and stuffed it into his delivery pouch. That helped a little. He was a bit chilly in just a T-shirt, but at least he didn't have the company's name in big letters across his back. He wished he could take the pants off too, but he wasn't going out on the street in his underwear.

He pulled the bicycle out from behind the dumpster. He wished he could just leave it there. But, if the bicycle got hauled away with the garbage—Never mind the guy in the black Jaguar, his boss would kill him for sure!

He pushed the bicycle to the end of the alley and looked up and down the street. No sign of a black sports car. No sign of the guy in the business suit. Just normal people going by on a normal afternoon. He got on the bicycle and pedaled down the sidewalk in the opposite direction from his apartment.

*   *   *

Five minutes later, the phone rang in the Little Friends Day Care Center where Heather worked.

"Heather, it's for you," called out Mrs. Santos, the director of the center. "It sounds like that young man of yours."

"Justin?" Heather said when she came to the phone. "Is that you? You were so strange on the phone last night! What was going on? Where are you now?"

"Look out the window," Justin said. "I'm across the street."

Heather turned around so that she could see out the window. At first she didn't see anyone. Then she noticed that the phone booth on the corner had a bicycle leaning against it. Inside the phone booth, through the glass, she could see someone waving. "Is that you in the phone booth?" she asked. "Why don't you just come in? Mrs. Santos doesn't mind."

"No, I can't come in. It wouldn't be safe. I don't want anyone to see you with me."

"Justin, what on earth are you talking about? Why don't you want anyone to see you with me? Justin, talk to me! What is going on?"

"I can't tell you," Justin said. "But I'm in trouble, and I need your help. Can you loan me enough money for a bus ticket?"

"A bus ticket? To where?"

"Anywhere! I just have to get out of town!"

"Justin, what has happened? You can tell me!" Heather wailed.

Around her, the children had stopped playing and were looking at her. One little girl with a red ribbon in her hair began to cry softly. Mrs. Santos was walking toward her. Her face showed a mixture of worrying about Heather and worrying about the children.

"Heather, dear," she said, "the children are beginning to get upset. Do you think you should take this call in my office?"

"Justin, tell me what is going on!" Heather demanded. "Quick! You're getting me in trouble here!"

"Look, someone has been following me," Justin said. "Someone busted up my apartment yesterday. I don't know why. But I don't want to get you involved. I don't want to put you in danger!"

"Well, Justin, it looks like I *am* involved," Heather said, "whether you like it or not! If you're being followed, you need to get off the street, especially with that bicycle! Come down the alley and into the day care center the back way. You can leave the bicycle in the storeroom in back of the kitchen. I'll come through the other way and let you in. Okay?"

"Okay," Justin said.

He didn't want to admit it, even to himself, but this was just what he was hoping Heather would do.

*   *   *

Later that afternoon they were sitting around Mrs. Grasso's kitchen table, sipping big glasses of lemonade. Justin looked around the room at the pots of flowers on the windowsill and the shiny pans hanging from a rack on the ceiling. There were pictures of small children—probably Mrs. Grasso's grandchildren—stuck to the refrigerator with little magnets. There were a dozen cookbooks lined up on the counter. She had tidy piles of coupons all ready for a trip to the store. It was cozy in the kitchen, the way a kitchen should be. The way he remembered his mother's kitchen before his father left.

Heather thought Mrs. Grasso's apartment might be

safer than hers. It had a private entrance off the alley where no one could see them going in. And Mrs. Grasso was just as happy as she could be to have them there. *She must be lonely,* Justin thought. *Those grandchildren must live a long way away.*

Mrs. Grasso had taken half of a chocolate cake from the bread box and was cutting it into slices. She brought Justin a large slice on a pretty blue plate that said "Souvenir of Niagara Falls" around the outside edge. His mother would have liked that plate. He felt right at home.

He stuck his fork into the cake and lifted a big chunk to his mouth. He inhaled the smell of chocolate before he put the cake into his mouth. It tasted pretty good, but it was slightly dried out. He peeked over at the cake where it sat on the counter, wondering how long it had been sitting in the bread box. Mrs. Grasso lived all alone except for that stupid poodle. Right now it was sitting on a big cushion in the corner of the room and glaring at Justin. He imagined Mrs. Grasso cutting herself one slice of cake every evening after supper. How long would it take her to eat half a cake?

"This is great cake!" Justin said loudly. He took another big bite and quickly washed it down with a big swallow of lemonade. "I don't know how long it's been since I've had homemade cake!"

Mrs. Grasso smiled broadly as she brought Heather a slice of cake on a bright green plate. "I'm glad you're enjoying it," she said. "I could give Heather the recipe. She should be collecting recipes of all your favorite dishes. After all, good cooking is the best way to make a marriage last. A girl needs to be able to make her husband happy! I mean—" She gave Heather a huge wink. "I mean, her best fellow, of course!"

Heather bent her face over her slice of cake to hide her blush. Justin took another big drink of lemonade and choked down another chunk of the cake. The poodle turned around on its pillow and thumped itself down again, never taking its eyes off Justin.

"So this man gave you a package, and you gave the package to Hugo," Heather said. "You don't know if Hugo gave the package to the Public Works office or not."

"Right," Justin said. "Hugo never came back to his apartment last night. At least I don't think so."

"Well, you don't have to worry about *that*," Heather said, smiling. "Knowing good old Hugo, he probably just forgot where his apartment was."

Justin did his best to laugh. He knew that Heather was just trying to make him feel better. He just hoped that Hugo really hadn't come home. He hoped that Hugo hadn't been in there, lying on the floor of his apartment, silent and still—like Albert Worth.

He shook his head to clear it. Heather was saying, "Mrs. Grasso, can I use your phone book?"

"Of course, dear. It's just over there, on the little table under the phone."

Heather looked up a number in the book, then dialed it. "Hello, is this the Public Works office?" she asked in a voice that sounded more like it belonged to a middle-aged woman. "Is this the office where Albert Worth worked? Yes, I was very sorry to hear about his death. This is Rosa Smith, from the City Water Department. We have a question—it's very important. Was a small package delivered to Mr. Worth's office yesterday morning? When we sent it, we hadn't heard yet about Mr. Worth. The package would have been delivered by hand, first thing yesterday morning. It was a computer disk of information for Mr. Worth to check, very important—" She stopped for a moment, listening. "Yes, if you could check—"

Heather glanced over at Justin. He was sitting in his chair, staring at her with his mouth hanging open. Heather blushed again. "I was in a lot of plays when I was in high school," she whispered. Then she was listening to the phone again. "I see," she said. "No one remembers a delivery? Well, thank you so much for checking."

She hung up the phone. "The package never got there yesterday morning," she told Justin. "And, of course, the office was closed all afternoon, for the—um—funeral."

Justin sighed. He pushed his plate away. He didn't think he could get the last dry bite of cake down his throat. "How am I going to find Hugo?" he asked.

"Well, let's phone him, and see if he's come back," Heather said. "What's his number?"

"I don't know. I never needed to call him. He was just always around."

Heather picked up the phone book again. "I'll look him up. What's his last name?"

"That's just the trouble. I don't know his last name."

"Oh, that's right." Heather put down the phone book, picked up the cake plates, and carried them over to the counter. "Well, then let's go over to your building and knock on his door." She saw Justin's startled look and smiled. "It's dark now. No one will see us. And just to be sure, we can go in disguise. Mrs. Grasso, could we borrow a couple of your sweaters?"

*   *   *

Justin and Heather walked down the street, trying not to walk too fast, being careful to stay out of the light from the street lamps. Justin felt very bulky—and much too warm—in two of Mrs. Grasso's sweaters, one on top of the other. He wasn't sure that they were much of a disguise, but he didn't take them off.

No traffic moved along Justin's street. No shiny black cars were parked anywhere nearby. Quickly they slipped in through the front door of his building and up the stairs.

They knocked on Hugo's door. No one answered. All was quiet in Hugo's apartment.

"If only his apartment weren't so high up. If only we could see in the window," Heather said.

Justin knew what she was thinking. If they could see in the window, they'd know if Hugo was in there— dead. "I guess I could go up the fire escape," he said. "Hugo's apartment is right above mine, so it should be on the same fire escape."

"That's a great idea!" Heather said. "We can go out through your window. Let's go!"

As Justin followed her down the stairs to his own door, he thought, *What do you mean WE?* Heather had always been the one worrying about how dangerous his job was. Now she wanted to sneak into his apartment and climb up the fire escape! He was seeing a whole new side of Heather that he had never seen before. And he liked it.

He was looking forward to learning more about her. If they lived through tonight.

CHAPTER 5

"Sshh, quiet!" Justin felt very strange, sneaking into his own apartment in the dark like a robber in his own home.

Carefully they sneaked across the room to the kitchen corner, moved the chairs, and lifted the table out from under the window. Justin stepped into the spot where the table had been and pushed up against the sash. It wouldn't move.

"When is the last time you had this window open?" Heather whispered.

"I don't know if I've ever had it open," Justin whispered back. "I guess it's a good thing there's never been a fire!"

He tapped all around the glass, rattled the sash, and gave a mighty heave. Suddenly, with a terrible squeak, the window lifted. Justin and Heather both dove for the floor and crouched huddled together, waiting for shots or footsteps or shouting voices.

Nothing happened.

Feeling very silly, they stood up again. In all the noises of the city around them, what was one squeaky window? "I don't know what we have to be so afraid of," Justin said.

Heather giggled. "Look at us, sneaking around like a couple of jerks. Come on, let's get out on that fire escape. Do you have the flashlight?"

"I've got it right here," Justin said, holding it up. "I'll go first."

He climbed out onto the fire escape, trying not to look down through the bars. He didn't really mind heights, but it was kind of creepy to look down three stories right through what he was standing on. He helped Heather out through the window until she was standing next to him.

He felt a slight breeze ruffle his hair. The sound of cars passing in the street below sounded different up here. They could hear voices in the rooms below and around them. Somewhere in the building a baby was crying.

As Justin began to move up the ladder, the fire escape shook under his weight and clanged against the side of the building. "Sshh!" Heather said. She sounded nervous again.

Justin drew himself up another rung and another, trying to keep himself steady so the ladder wouldn't shake. It wasn't easy, climbing with the flashlight in his hand. The little breeze ruffled his hair again. The cold air blew down the back of his neck, making him shiver.

He felt the ladder jiggle as Heather climbed up a rung behind him. Somewhere below them, the baby was still crying. Why didn't someone pick up the poor thing?

Rung by rung, they climbed the ladder. After what seemed like hours, they stood side by side on the metal grate under Hugo's window.

"Go ahead," Heather whispered, "shine the flashlight in the window."

Justin swallowed. He lifted the flashlight to the glass and turned it on. Beside him, Heather gasped, "Someone has busted up *his* apartment too!"

Justin peered through the window and shone the light around the kitchen. "No, I don't think so," he said. "It's a mess, but it's the usual mess. This is just how Hugo lives."

The table under the window was piled with things: dirty dishes, empty cereal boxes, magazines, dirty clothes, one shoe. Beyond it, the cupboard doors were standing open. A few boxes and cans of food stood here and there on the shelves, looking lonely. The front of the refrigerator was covered with layers of papers and pictures cut out of magazines. Some of them were bent and ragged-looking as if they'd been there a long time.

Justin shone the flashlight further into the room. He could pick out the bed—more like a big heap of blankets—and the closet. The closet was standing open, and there were more clothes on the floor than there were on hangers. A TV sat on a table in the corner. Near it sat a computer with a printer. On the back wall was a CD player with huge speakers. A big case held hundreds of CDs, all standing neatly in rows.

Heather whispered, "Are you *sure* this place hasn't been trashed?"

"Oh, it's been trashed all right, but only by Hugo," Justin whispered back. He shone the light back to the closet, saying, "See? *Some* of Hugo's clothes are on hangers. The big apes that searched my place didn't leave *anything* alone!" He switched the light to the CD case. "Look at his CDs. He keeps them in perfect order, alphabetical by group. He loves his CDs."

Justin could feel himself smiling in the dark. He felt so much better that he wanted to hug Heather. He wanted to laugh out loud! Hugo's apartment was its usual mess—just the way Hugo had left it. And there was no dead body lying on the floor.

"But where *is* he?" Heather whispered, as if she knew what he was thinking.

"I don't know. I don't know him well enough to know where he would go."

"Shine the light on the kitchen again," Heather said, "and maybe we can find a clue."

Justin moved the flashlight beam slowly across the kitchen table. "Isn't that one of your bowls?" Heather asked.

"Yeah, he borrowed it the other day. Oh, look, there's my can opener. When he gets back, I'll have to—" He stopped. Just because Hugo wasn't lying dead inside his apartment didn't mean he was ever coming back.

"Shine the light on the refrigerator," Heather said.

Justin did. They strained their eyes looking at the different papers that were stuck up with magnets.

"Wait," Heather said, "here's something!" She grabbed Justin's wrist to move the light to a small poster stuck in the upper corner. They both peered at the poster. There was a lot of print that was too small to see, but they could read the words at the top:

COMPUTER SHOW
Monday through Thursday, June 2-5
Grand Ballroom
Hanover Hotel

"What's today?" Justin asked.

"It's Tuesday, the third. Well, maybe by now it's Wednesday," Heather said. "Do you think he might have gone to the show?"

"Yeah, he's really into computers."

"But I thought he'd just started a new job," Heather said.

Justin shrugged. "It's worth a try. The Hanover Hotel—that's downtown. There'll be a lot of people there, so we should be safe enough."

"Well," Heather said, "speaking of being safe, let's get off this fire escape."

"Right," Justin said, switching off the flashlight and shoving it into his pocket. He stuck his foot down through the hole in the grate, felt around for the first rung of the ladder, and stepped down into the darkness. The fire escape shook and clanged against the front of the building. He took another step and another and another.

It seemed extra dark. A lot of the lights were out now in the apartments around them. It must be very late. He realized that the baby had stopped crying. A car passed on the street below them, and then all was quiet again.

Suddenly the fire escape rattled and clanged again as Heather began to move down the rungs. It sounded so loud that Justin expected to see windows opening and people sticking their heads out to shout at them to be quiet.

They moved slowly downward in the dark, struggling to be quiet, toward the darker dark of Justin's open window below them. When another car passed by down on the street, Justin held still, waiting for it to go by. Heather stepped down until she was just above him on the ladder.

The car had slowed down. It pulled into a parking space across the street and stopped. Two men got out. They walked across the street toward Justin's apartment building, moving smoothly, like big cats.

There was no question in Justin's mind as to who they were. He'd never seen them before, but he would know them anywhere. He watched them trot up the front steps below him and into the building.

The window! If they came into his apartment, they'd see the open window! Then they'd look out and check the fire escape!

He judged the distance to the ground. If he'd been by himself, he might have been able to make it to the ground. But not with Heather. There wasn't time for both of them.

He looked up. The fire escape didn't go all the way to the roof. It stopped at the window above Hugo's. They were trapped.

Faintly, through the open window, he could hear footsteps drumming on the staircase. Then he could hear the men working on the door to his apartment. He stuck out his foot and pushed down on the window sash until the window closed almost all the way.

Inside the apartment, the door burst open. A beam

of light moved quickly across the window and was gone. The men must be using flashlights—to look for what? The package? Him?

"Quick!" Heather whispered above him. "We've got to get down!"

"Sshh, don't move!" Justin hissed, pressing his hand down on her foot to keep her still. "We'd never make it!"

They hung in silence on the ladder. Just below them the window gleamed for an instant as the flashlights passed in front of it. *What are the men doing?* Justin wondered. *Are they searching for the package all over again?*

No, they must have been looking for him. They searched for only a minute or two before they realized that what they were looking for wasn't there. And this time, they were angry.

Thud! Something fell to the floor inside the apartment. Crash! Something heavy fell over, followed by the sound of breaking glass. *I'll bet that was my TV!* Justin thought. Thud! Thud! Thud! *My bookcase!* Justin gritted his teeth together to keep himself from shouting out loud. He wanted to climb down to the window, jump in, and grab those guys. Closer, in the kitchen now, more glass breaking—all his dishes! A light gleamed. *That's the refrigerator light,* Justin thought. *They're dumping the stuff out of my refrigerator!* He felt as if he was standing by, watching himself get beat up. *Please, not my bicycle! Please, please, please, not my bicycle!*

The neighbors downstairs would hear the noise. They'd call the police! But the men were fast. In not much more than a minute the sounds of destruction stopped. Justin heard their footsteps moving away toward the door.

At that moment, the flashlight fell out of his pocket. Clang! It hit a rung near his feet. Whang-whang! It hit the grate below the window, bounced once, and dropped through the hole to the grate below. Clang-clang! The whole fire escape rang like a bell.

"Hey!" said a rough voice inside the apartment. "What was that?"

"Something outside on the fire escape!" another voice answered. Heavy footsteps rushed toward the window. "Look, this window's open! I'll bet the little creep saw us coming, and he's out on the fire escape!"

"Up, up!" Justin shouted at Heather, but she was already scampering up the ladder in the dark. He was right behind her, reaching up and grabbing at each rung almost before her foot left it.

With a grinding squeak, the window opened below them. "There!" shouted a voice. "There he is!" Something whistled by Justin's ear and pinged off the side of the building. A split second later there was the muffled *whump* of a gun with a silencer. Justin froze, too frightened to move.

"Get back, you idiot!" snarled the other voice. "The boss wants him alive! Dead men can't answer questions!" Then the fire escape shook as someone climbed out onto the grate.

"Justin, come on!" Heather shrieked.

Justin lunged upward to where Heather was huddled in front of Hugo's window. "I can't open it!" she wailed.

Justin didn't try. He threw his shoulder against the glass. The whole pane smashed across Hugo's kitchen table. Justin shoved the table aside with his foot and leaped into the room. He grabbed Heather by the arms and yanked her in after him.

Skittering in the bits of broken glass, they dashed across the room toward the door. Justin fumbled with the lock. *Come on!* he told himself. *Come on!*

"Hey, you!" the man on the fire escape shouted. "We've got you!" He heaved himself in through the broken window.

The lock on the door snapped open. Justin yanked open the door, pushed Heather through it, and jumped through after her. He slammed the door shut again and leaned against it. The stairwell echoed with the thunder of heavy footsteps coming toward them.

"Up!" shouted Justin.

He and Heather pounded up the staircase. They had no idea where they would go. They just knew they had to run and run and run.

They got to the next landing. There was only one more floor to go, and then they would be trapped in the upstairs hall.

Suddenly a door popped open. A small man in wrinkled pajamas leaned out to look at them. His white hair, standing up on end around the bald top of his head, shone in the light from the room behind him. "What's the matter with you people?" he snapped. "Do you know what *time* it is?"

"Get back!" Justin shouted. He grabbed the man and shoved him backward through the door. He pushed him into a chair just inside the door and turned to yank Heather into the room.

"Hey!" the man screeched as Justin slammed the door shut.

"Call the police!" Heather shouted at the man. "Call 9-1-1!"

"I have already called them," the man said with a strange smile on his face, "and they are on the way at this moment." Then he lifted his hand from his pajama pocket and pointed a gun at Justin. "And you two will wait for them outside."

As he stood up, he snapped off the safety on the gun. His thin, wrinkled finger tightened on the trigger. "Outside," he said again. "Get out. Now!"

CHAPTER
6

Justin stared into the barrel of the gun that was pointed right at his face. It was like a cruel, black eye looking back at him. The gun did not waver. The little old man kept it pointed steadily at him.

"If you are thinking that I can't shoot this thing because I'm old, you're wrong," the old man said in a firm voice. "I was in the army for a lot of years, and I know exactly what I'm doing. I'm not afraid to shoot. So get out, *now*."

"But you don't understand! I'm Justin Cobb, and I live downstairs," Justin said. "There are two men out there in the hall who broke into my apartment and busted everything up. Heather and I were hiding on the fire escape." Justin was talking faster and faster, sweating in the warm, stuffy air of the old man's apartment. "Now they've found us! They're after us! You've got to help us!"

When he stopped to take a breath, he heard the quiet footsteps out in the hallway, coming toward the door behind him. Justin's eyes bulged wildly as he put his finger up in front of his mouth to beg the old man to be quiet.

The old man was not impressed. "Let me guess. You were making a drug deal, and something went wrong," he said. "I've been living in this city a long time, and I've seen a lot. But it's not going to happen in *my* apartment, not while I've got this." Holding the gun straight out in front of him with both arms stiff, he took one step closer to Justin. "You've got until the count of three to open that door and get out, or I'll shoot. One."

"Oh, please!" Justin whispered. The footsteps had stopped. Only the door, one thin piece of wood, separated him from the two men. "Please—"

"Two," said the old man.

"Wait!" Justin cried. Out on the street, he heard the thin, high wail of a police siren. Were they coming here? Or would they pass by?

The siren came closer, closer, and blue lights flashed through the front window. The siren cut off as if it had been choked. Car doors slammed.

"The police have arrived," the old man said. "You may go out into the hall to meet them." The gun barrel stared into Justin's face as the old man took another step closer. "Open that door and get out."

Justin's hand reached back as if it were working by itself and found the doorknob. His other hand fumbled with the lock until the bolt snapped back. The door cracked, and a breath of cool air from the hall wafted by Justin.

He listened, but there was no sound from the hall. He pulled the door open and looked out. The hall was empty. Where were the two men? Around the corner? Or down the stairs, in the hall below, waiting?

Now new footsteps echoed up the stairwell, and two faces appeared under the dim light of the stairs, climbing toward them. Two blue uniforms came into the light. Justin's knees felt weak with relief. The police! For the moment, at least, everything would be all right.

"Police officers!" called a voice from the stairs below them. "Are you the person who called in a complaint?"

"I did, Officer," said the old man. He stepped out into the hall, never taking his gun off Justin. "I heard these young people running up the fire escape. They broke out the window of the apartment below me and went in. Then they tried to break into my apartment. I've been holding them until you arrived. And yes, I have a permit for this gun, and I know how to use it."

The police officers walked toward them. One was a big man with heavy-lidded eyes. Behind him was his partner, a thin woman wearing bright red lipstick. Both of them smiled at the old man. "I guess you've got them for sure," said the first officer. "Good work, Pops!"

"Hmph!" the old man snorted. He stepped back into his apartment and slammed the door.

The policeman had pulled out a set of handcuffs as he came at Justin, and behind him, the policewoman had her hand on her gun.

"Wait!" Justin said. "We didn't break into that apartment! I mean, we did, but—"

"He lives downstairs," Heather said, "and we were on the fire escape because—"

"Well, because—" Justin said. How could they explain this?

"We were in Justin's apartment downstairs," Heather said firmly, "just minding our own business, and two men broke in. We were scared, and we ran out onto the fire escape. Didn't you see the men when you came up the stairs?"

"No, we didn't see anyone. No one at all. You're sure *you* saw these two men?" the policeman asked. "Or are you on something?"

"They busted up Justin's apartment!" Heather cried. "And when we got out on the fire escape, one of them shot at us!"

The policeman's eyebrows lifted. "Let's have a look at this apartment of yours," he said to Justin. "Then you'd better be able to tell us why these guys were after you."

* * *

Justin's apartment was a mess. Under the glare of the overhead light, it looked like a newspaper picture of a house after a tornado. Justin could hardly believe that the men had been in the room only for a minute or two. They had hit everything.

The TV was on its face in a heap of broken glass. All the dishes and glasses in the kitchen were broken. The food from the refrigerator was mixed in with the glass. His clothes were rags. His books and magazines were torn and thrown everywhere.

And his bicycle, his beautiful racing bicycle! The frame had been jammed under the toilet in the bathroom and bent almost double. The men had used his lamp to twist the spokes out of the back wheel. The front wheel was lying on top of the stove in the kitchen. Justin didn't want to know what they'd been planning to do with that.

The officers looked carefully at the damage. They checked the apartment door where the men had scratched the lock getting in. They woke up the super to let them into Hugo's apartment. Justin had to convince them that Hugo's apartment had not been trashed too. He was getting tired of explaining Hugo's lifestyle.

"Okay," the policeman said when they were finished, "these two guys broke in, trashed your place, shot at you, and ran off when they heard us coming. I've got that part. But you haven't answered the big question: *Why?*"

"I keep telling you, I don't know why!" Justin said.

"You must have done something to get them started," the other officer said.

"I've never seen them before!" Justin said. *But I would have known them anywhere,* he thought.

As the policeman closed his notebook, he stared hard at Justin for a long moment, then at Heather. "We're going to be keeping an eye on you two," he said.

Somewhere in the building, the baby started to cry.

*   *   *

Justin spent the night, what was left of it, on Mrs. Grasso's couch, and Heather stayed in a friend's apartment in the next building. They hadn't dared stay at Justin's place after the police left. Justin was beginning to wonder if he'd ever be able to stay there again.

In the morning they felt heavy but stronger after eating a huge breakfast cooked by Mrs. Grasso. After much discussion, they both decided to call in sick to work. Then they could head downtown and look for Hugo at the computer show.

The Hanover Hotel was a tall new building on the widest street downtown. The building was mostly glass. The huge front door, complete with a doorman in uniform, was meant to impress people as they came toward it.

It did. Justin and Heather, both dressed in whatever clothes they could borrow, felt completely out of place. They slipped through the front door in the middle of a crowd of well-dressed businessmen and looked around them. They were afraid to ask anyone for help. Finally they found signs pointing them to the Grand Ballroom.

The Grand Ballroom was huge, and it was completely packed with people and computers. Little booths had been set up in rows, row upon row, as far as they could see. People pushed their way into the booths to look at the latest computers or squeezed by each other to get into the next booth.

"Even if Hugo is here, how will we ever find him?" Justin asked.

Heather sighed. "We've got to try," she said.

"I'll keep looking to the right, and you look to the left," Justin said. Hand in hand so as to keep together, they pushed their way into the crowd.

The computer show had everything—every kind of computer with every kind of program. Justin kept wanting to stop and look at the displays, but Heather kept him moving. They worked their way up one row of booths and down the next. They looked into each booth and tried to keep their eyes on the crowd too. "This isn't going to work," Justin muttered. "He could be right next to us, and we wouldn't even see him." They pushed on up the third row.

"One more row to go," Justin said.

"Then we should work our way back again," Heather said. "He could be moving around."

"Yeah," Justin sighed. They pushed on. They got to the back corner of the ballroom, which was just as crowded as the front. There had been no sign of Hugo. "This is useless," Justin said.

"But it's our only chance," Heather said, "so keep looking."

They kept looking. And suddenly, as they were coming up to the front door again, they saw him.

Hugo was sitting on a stool in a booth, tapping away on a computer keyboard. A man standing next to him was talking away, telling him all about the computer. It was clear that Hugo was not listening. He was in a world of his own.

"Hugo!" Justin yelled. "We've been looking everywhere for you!"

Hugo turned his head, smiled in Justin's direction, and went back to his keyboard.

"Hugo, I have to talk to you!" Justin said. He grabbed Hugo by the arm and pulled him off the stool.

"Hey, man, what's the problem?" Hugo said. "This computer was just getting interesting!"

Hugo was wearing the same clothes that Justin had seen him wearing Monday morning. This time they were definitely wrinkled. In fact, they looked as if he had been sleeping in them. His hair was standing away from his head in wisps. He looked tired but happy.

"Hugo, remember that package I gave you on Sunday? You were going to take it to the Public Works office for me on Monday morning on your way to work. Remember?"

Hugo's eyes blinked. He looked puzzled. Then his face broke into a smile. "Oh, yeah, I remember!"

"Well?"

"Well, what?" Hugo asked.

"Did you deliver it? Did you take the package to the Public Works office?"

"I don't know," Hugo said. "I don't remember. Oh, hi, Heather, I didn't see you. How's it going?"

"Hugo!" Justin wanted to grab him and shake him until he rattled. "Hugo, you put the package in your pocket. You were going to take it to the Public Works office on South 13th Street."

"In my pocket?" Hugo asked. "Oh, that's right. I was wondering what this was." He put his hand into his jacket pocket and pulled out the package.

"You've got it!" Justin yelled. He threw his arms around Hugo and hugged him. Then he hugged Heather. "You've got it!" he yelled again.

"So what is this thing?" Hugo asked. While he spoke, he was tearing open the package.

"No! Don't touch it!" Justin yelled. He tried to grab the package away from Hugo, but it was too late. Hugo had the package open. He tipped it and a computer disk slipped into his hand.

"Well, well, look what we have here. Let's try it out," Hugo said. Before Justin could stop him, he sat down and shoved the disk into the slot in the computer in front of him. He tapped a few keys on the keyboard, and the computer screen filled with words. In spite of himself, Justin leaned forward to look. The words didn't mean much to him. They looked like lists in some kind of code.

Hugo tapped a few more keys. "This has been coded," he muttered, "but I've never met a code I couldn't break. We'll just copy this little baby onto the hard drive—Good—Now I'll just see how it goes with this program—"

Justin watched closely over his shoulder as the computer screen flashed to a set of icons. The screen changed again as Hugo moved and clicked the computer mouse.

"So Hugo, where have you been the last two days?" Justin asked him while he worked.

"Oh, right here, mostly. I came down after work on Monday, and I met some guys who have a booth back there somewhere." Hugo waved a hand toward the middle of the room. "We were playing some computer games, and next thing I knew, it was morning. I hadn't slept at all, so I called in sick and slept in their room in the hotel. Same thing last night. They've got some great new games. Then—What day is it today?"

Justin looked at Heather. He'd been worried sick about Hugo, and all the time Hugo had been here at the hotel, playing computer games!

"Now we're getting somewhere," Hugo said, while his hand sent the mouse through quick, tiny moves. "I'll just hide this over here for a moment—" The screen went blank.

"What happened?" Justin asked.

"You've got some pretty hot stuff here," Hugo told him, "and I think you'd better—" He looked up at Justin and stopped. Justin's face was white. His mouth was set in a thin line. His eyes were staring toward the front door.

When Hugo and Heather turned to see what he was looking at, they couldn't understand why Justin looked so scared. The man coming toward them didn't look like anyone special. He was in his forties and wearing a business suit. Except for his build, which made him look stronger than most people his age, he looked like anyone else at the computer show.

"Well, well," the man said, "if it isn't Mr. Cobb."

CHAPTER 7

Justin didn't have time to think. He had to move fast.

"Hello, sir!" he said in a loud voice to the man in the business suit. He hoped his voice didn't sound as shaky as he felt. "I've been looking for you." He stepped forward away from the booth to try to make it look as if he had just been walking down the aisle. He stuck his hand behind his back and waved it frantically to tell Heather and Hugo to get away. Had they understood his signal? He didn't dare look back at them to see.

The man came toward him through the crowd, staring straight into Justin's eyes. His muscles bunched under his suit coat. His arms swung easily at his sides, hands open and ready for action. Justin could almost feel those hands grabbing for his throat. If the guy found out they'd been looking at his disk, he'd probably rip all three of them apart right there in the hotel!

For an instant, the man's eyes flicked away from Justin's, as if he were looking at something over Justin's shoulder. In the next instant, his eyes had locked again on Justin's.

He smiled. The smile, showing perfect white teeth, stayed in his mouth. The eyes were cold. "So you've been looking for me? That's good. Because I believe you have something that doesn't belong to you."

"Yes, sir." Justin forced himself to take another step closer to the man, away from the booth. Had Heather and Hugo managed to move away into the crowd? Was that what the man had been looking at? *Keep talking,* he told himself. *Keep the guy's attention!* "I mean, I did have it, that package of yours," he said loudly, "but—"

"You *did* have it?" The man's smile faded, leaving his mouth set and hard. "And where is it now? You'd better know, because if you don't—" The man's hands clenched themselves into fists. "If you don't give it to me right now, I'll—"

Justin didn't wait to find out what the man had in mind for him. He whirled around and sprinted down the aisle.

"Hey! Come back here!" the man shouted behind him. "Stop! Someone stop him!"

Hands reached out from the crowd to grab Justin. Before anyone could take hold of him, he was past them. He dodged around groups of startled people, running, running as he had never run before.

He took the corner so fast that his feet began to slip out from under him. Fighting to get his balance again, he was running down the next aisle. He slammed into a middle-aged man and sent him flying, but he never looked back. He ran on, stretching to get the most out of every step.

His mind raced, trying to figure out which way to dodge in the crowded aisle. He had to guess which way the people would jump when they looked up and saw him coming. His heart pounded in his ears. Time seemed to slow down so that every step was in slow motion, like running through deep water.

Justin jerked himself sideways through a space between two booths and cut across the next aisle. The booth in front of him had a partition across the back that did not meet the floor, and Justin dove under it.

He popped up in the booth on the other side of the partition, behind a young woman in a blue dress. She screamed when Justin suddenly brushed against her. "Sshh!" he called to her. "It's okay!" He scrambled to his feet and leapt out into the last aisle.

Pushing his way toward him through the crowd was the man in the business suit. Justin whirled around to go the other way. Coming toward him were two men, shoving through the crowd. Their faces were hard. When they saw him, their eyes glittered.

Justin leapt forward into the booth on the other side of the aisle. Quick as a thought, his right foot was on a fancy red folding chair, his left foot was on the computer table, his hands were on the top of the partition, and he was over.

He dropped to the floor with a thump. He found himself in a sort of narrow alley between the last row of booths and the wall. In front of him was a door—unlocked. He was through it.

Then he was in a long hall with lots of doors on both sides, all closed. He dashed along the hall, trying some of the doors as he went by, but they all seemed to be locked. What was he going to do? It wasn't going to take those guys long to figure out where he'd gone.

And now he was trapped in this hall, like the target in a shooting gallery. He tried the door at the very end of the hall. It was locked too.

He could hear shouting in the Grand Ballroom, coming closer. He backed himself into the farther corner of the hall, trying to squeeze himself smaller.

The door next to him opened. Someone started to come out into the hall. He pushed the someone backward through the doorway in a tangle of arms and legs, pressed through himself, and shoved the door shut, all in the matter of an instant.

The place he had entered turned out to be the back corner of the hotel kitchen. And the someone he had pushed turned out to be a large woman of about fifty wearing a black waitress uniform with a white apron. "Well!" she huffed, smoothing down her apron and patting her hair. "What was *that* all about?" As she spoke, she reached for the door handle and began to pull on it.

"No!" Justin gasped, grabbing her hand and pulling it off the handle. "Don't go out there!"

The woman straightened herself up, and Justin realized that she was almost as tall as he was. "What is going on?" she demanded. "Why shouldn't I go out there?"

"The—um—the computer show is being held up!" Justin said. "There are men out there with guns!"

The woman lifted one eyebrow. "Oh, yes, I'm sure. Well, I think you'd better come with me and tell it to my good friend the security guard." With that she grabbed Justin by the back of the collar, almost lifted him off his feet, and started to march him toward the middle of the huge kitchen.

"It's true!" Justin said, trying to break free without shoving the waitress again. "I mean—the men do have guns!"

"Oh, yes, the guns. Stop your wiggling, young man!" the woman said. "You just come right over here—"

"There he is!" shouted a voice behind them. "Hang onto him, lady!"

The woman half turned toward the voice. Justin twisted out of her grip and sprinted across the kitchen. He dodged around tables and counters, around men in white uniforms and tall white hats, around people carrying trays of food. As he ran, part of his brain was thinking, *In the movies, people are always being chased through hotel kitchens. This isn't really happening to me!*

"Stop him!" "Get him!" Voices rang out all over the room. Hands reached out to grab him. It *was* happening to him.

At the far end of a counter in front of him, three young men in white uniforms bunched together, ready, waiting for him. His mind raced. *They don't want me to go this way*, he thought. *That must be the way to the outside door!*

He ran right at them.

They didn't move. They stood shoulder to shoulder, hands ready to grab him, watching him come. He put his head down and went right into the middle of them.

"Oof!" someone croaked as Justin's head sank into his stomach. The three men went down in a knot of white uniforms. Justin scrambled right over the top of them. He felt their hands grasping at him. He jerked himself free, scrambled to his feet, and raced for the door. In a moment, he was outside.

He was in an alley. To the left was a dead end, the wall of a building. Not that way! To the right, dumpsters overflowing with big plastic bags stood along the side of the hotel. No good—the men would look for him there first.

Beyond the dumpsters, at the end of the alley, was the main street. And on the street, waiting to cross to the other side, was a teenage boy with a bicycle. "Yes!" Justin cried. He dashed down the alley.

Behind him, the kitchen door slammed open. "There he is!" someone shouted. "Get him!" Feet pounded down the alley behind him.

Justin was already across the wide sidewalk, and his hands were around the handlebars of the bicycle. The boy was so startled by his sudden appearance that he let go of the bicycle and jumped back. Justin flung himself onto the bicycle and launched himself out into the street. "Hey!" shouted the boy behind him. "Hey! What do you think you're doing?"

Justin didn't have time to answer him. His feet found the pedals. His legs pumped and his hands steered as if they were working on their own. He seemed to have eyes all the way around his head as he ducked in and through the line of cars without glancing at them.

He could hear voices shouting behind him. He shot between two cars coming through the intersection. He went up over the corner of the sidewalk on the other side of the street and down into the traffic moving away from the hotel. He wove in and out of the line of cars. He moved up as fast as he could and zipped through the next intersection just as the light turned red.

That should slow them down some! Justin bent low over the handlebars, set the bicycle's gears as high as he could, and pedaled. He passed three cars on the right. Then he cut behind a semi truck and zipped by it on the left by riding down the yellow line in the middle of the street. He was moving today! If his boss could only see him now!

He cut left at the next intersection, pedaling so fast that he almost laid the bicycle on its side. He wished he had his own bicycle. It would sure take the corners better than this thing! Then he remembered what the men had done to his bicycle, and anger jolted through him like an electric shock. He leaned forward and pedaled faster, faster.

He glanced up at the buildings he was passing. He was on North Third Street, coming up to Grant Street. At least the map he carried with him in his head was still working.

But where was he going to go? Should he bicycle all the way across the city to his own neighborhood? Or would he be safer if he dumped the bicycle and hopped on a bus?

And what about Heather? And Hugo? Had they gotten away safely? Or were the men holding them, trying to find out where he might go?

They'd be safe as long as the men needed them. After that—He didn't want to think about what might happen after that. He had to stay loose out here in the city. It might be the only way Heather and Hugo would stay alive.

He turned right onto Grant Street and pedaled with the traffic for three blocks. Then he turned onto North Sixth Street and zigzagged up to to North 14th. Then he worked his way back to Sixth Street again. Ahead of him, the light was turning red. He bounced up onto the sidewalk to make the right turn, groaning as the bicycle thumped over the curb. He'd been riding hard for over an hour. He was getting tired. Very tired.

He rode down Ellis Street, keeping pace with the traffic, looking for a place where he could get out of sight and rest a bit. There was no way the men could have followed him through all the turns he had made. All he had to do was find a place to hide for awhile, and everything would be all right.

He was passing a store with a big glass window. By some kind of instinct, he glanced at the glass as he passed by. He saw himself and the line of cars he was in. Reflected in the glass, three cars behind him, was a black Jaguar.

A hot wave of fear shot through him. His lungs were on fire; his legs were burning. He felt too weak to move. He couldn't feel his feet beyond the burning in his legs, but they seemed to be locked onto the bicycle's pedals. The bicycle rolled along with the movement of the traffic, coasting.

Suddenly he just wanted it to be over. He wanted to pull over and stop, wait for the black Jaguar to catch up with him, let the men do whatever they wanted to him. He imagined himself rolling to a stop, letting the bicycle lean over, putting out a foot on the curb, just stopping. But, no! He couldn't stop! He had pulled Heather into this thing and now Hugo. He couldn't let them down!

He forced his legs to push down on the pedals. *Come on, body, let's go!* He ignored the ache in his muscles and concentrated on the movement—right, left, right—push, push, push—until he was moving smoothly again. Then, just before the corner, he slammed down on the pedal, cut between two parked cars, jerked up on the handlebars, and jumped the bicycle up onto the sidewalk. He dodged around hurrying businessmen, ladies with shopping bags waiting for the walk light, young men selling watches and neckties out of suitcases. Leaning low, he cut right around the corner.

Only then did he let himself look back. The black Jaguar was halfway through the intersection. Suddenly it slammed on the brakes. Horns blared and tires screamed as other cars swerved to avoid the Jaguar. The Jaguar's tires screamed as the car hauled itself around in a sharp right turn. After him.

Justin leaned into the pedals and streaked down the sidewalk. His heart pounded as if it would break right out of his chest, and his head beat out questions at the same time. How did they find him? Had the black Jaguar been behind him all this time? Or was it just his bad luck that they'd seen him?

He dodged in and out among the people who crowded the sidewalk. "Get out of my way!" he bellowed. How could people move so slowly? They stood there like cows, watching him come at them, too stupid to figure out which way to jump. "Watch out! Watch out! Get out of my way!"

He glanced left. The black Jaguar was pulling even with him. The dark-tinted side window was cranking down.

Now! He slammed the bicycle over and swung his right foot out onto the sidewalk. He grabbed the bicycle by the frame and spun around. In an instant he was pedaling back up the sidewalk in the other direction.

The people on the sidewalk shouted angrily at him, seeing him coming back. Two men jumped toward him

and tried to grab him. He swung wide around them
and kept pedaling. Behind him, horns blared again.
Then the sickening squeal of tires. Justin glanced back
over his shoulder. The black Jaguar was making a U-
turn in the middle of the street!

He pedaled harder than ever. His leg muscles
burned. There was a sharp pain like a knife in the small
of his back. He leaned far forward over the handlebars
and pedaled.

His only chance was to get around the next corner
ahead of the Jaguar and run into a department store.
Maybe he could hide in a changing room or under a
rack of clothes. He'd have to take the bicycle in with
him, or the men would spot it. He'd need plenty of
time to wrestle the bicycle in through the front door of
the store. Oh, how did the corner get so far away?

He glanced back. The Jaguar had made the turn. It
was coming again, up the other side of the street.
Justin whipped left around the corner. What street was
he on now? By instinct he dodged around the people
on the sidewalk while his eyes searched for a store with
an extra big door. He had to find one fast!

There! That big toy store! He could ditch the bicycle
among the new bicycles for sale! He dove down the
sidewalk toward the toy store. He was almost to it—
Suddenly the front door of the store opened. A flock of
children poured out onto the sidewalk. Too late Justin
saw the big yellow school bus pulling up to the curb.

He was hurtling toward the children. It was too late
to stop. He squeezed the brakes and laid the bicycle
over toward the right. He straightened up just as he
shot off the curb in front of the bus. The bicycle jolted
as it hit the street. The bus's tires scrunched on the

pavement, and the huge yellow hood loomed over him. He swerved out around the enormous left fender—

A flash of blue and silver—A car came out of nowhere, passing the bus. Justin saw the driver's startled face as he flew over the hood. The last thing he saw was the gray pavement rushing toward him.

CHAPTER 8

"Don't move him! Get back! Give him air!"

"Somebody call an ambulance!"

The voices boomed around Justin, echoing inside his head. The words didn't mean anything to him. The people's faces were a blur. His eyes fell shut again.

Then a siren, coming nearer, so loud—and suddenly cut off. Hands touching him. Someone speaking loudly, close to his face. "Can you hear me? Hey, buddy, can you hear me?"

Justin pried his eyes open. The light was so bright that it seemed to cut into his brain. In the middle of the light, a face loomed over him, waiting. "Yes, I hear you," Justin whispered.

Oh, his head hurt! He shut his eyes against the light. He wished all these people would just go away and let him rest. He'd open his eyes again sometime. Maybe next week—

"Careful! Looks like we have a head injury here," the voice said. "Get the back board."

Hands grasped both sides of his face so that he couldn't turn his head. Hands worked on every part of him, covering him, strapping him down. He didn't care. He wasn't really there. It wasn't really his body.

At last he felt himself being lifted. Oh, his poor head! He couldn't be there at all any more. He just had to go away.

*   *   *

Justin opened his eyes. He was lying in a bed. Nearby, a nurse was moving around.

He was in a hospital. He remembered being brought here, and the doctors checking him over. The memories were in bits and pieces, all jumbled together. It seemed as if there were something else he was supposed to remember, but he was just too tired.

His eyes slowly closed, and he slept again.

*   *   *

"Mr. Cobb! Wake up, Mr. Cobb. It's time for your supper."

Justin's eyes flew open. Supper! He struggled to sit up, but a hand pressed down on his chest. "Slowly, slowly, take it easy," the nurse was saying. "You've had a nasty bang on the head."

Justin lay back against the pillows. His head was throbbing. His eyes seemed to creak inside the sockets like an old barn door as he turned them toward the window. Yes, the sun was getting low. The day was almost gone.

The nurse pulled a table into position over his legs. Then she put a bowl and a glass on it. As he watched her, he tried to work out why he was here.

He had been at a computer show with Heather, looking for Hugo. Then the men came and chased him—on a bicycle. Now he remembered the bicycle. And the black Jaguar. And there was something about children, and a school bus—But how did he end up here?

"Eat your supper, now," the nurse was saying. "You need to get your strength back." She turned to go.

"Nurse!" Justin called her back. "What happened to me? Was I shot?"

The nurse laughed. "Shot? No, no. From what I've been told, you were on a bicycle and got hit by a car. You landed on your head."

"What kind of car?" Justin demanded. "Was it a black Jaguar?"

"Well, I have no idea what kind of car it was!" the nurse said. She looked at him with her head to one side. "Now why would it have to be a fancy car that hit you?"

"Never mind," Justin said quickly. Fear clutched again at his insides. He looked around him. He was wearing a hospital gown, and a white sheet covered his bare legs. An IV bag hanging above his head dripped a clear liquid into a tube that ended in a bandage on the back of his hand. How was he going to get out of here?

"Nurse," he called again, "where are my clothes?"

"They're all safe and sound in that closet over there." The nurse pointed to a narrow door beyond the foot of his bed. "Do you need something? Are you feeling all right? Is your head—?"

"No, I'm okay," Justin said. "Um—how much longer do I have to have this needle in my hand?"

The nurse looked at his chart. "Just as soon as that bag is finished, we can take the tubing off," she said. "That is, *if* you eat a good supper." Looking at him again to be sure he understood, she hurried out.

Justin looked again at the window. The sun had set, and it was beginning to get dark.

The men must know where he was. How hard would it be for them to follow the ambulance to this hospital? He had been surrounded by nurses and doctors all day, but now night was coming. There would be fewer people around. The hospital would get quiet. Sometime tonight, he was sure, the men would make their move.

He looked over at the man in the bed next to his. He was an old guy, happily eating his supper while he watched a game show on the TV on the opposite wall. "Hi, there," Justin said.

The man glanced over at him, then turned his eyes back to the TV. He didn't look at Justin again. Justin didn't care. He didn't want to make friends with the guy. He just needed the old man's clothes.

Justin looked at his supper. A bowl of soup and a glass of milk. How exciting! His stomach lurched at the thought of it, but he made himself drink every drop. He needed that needle out of his arm. And he would rather not have to pull it out himself.

*   *   *

It seemed to take forever for the IV bag to empty itself. Justin lay there watching the bag drip, drip, drip into the tube. He knew he should be using the time to rest up, but he was too nervous to lie still. Every time someone went by in the hallway he tensed up, wondering if the next person through his doorway would have a gun in his hand. What would he do—hit the guy with his IV bag? In the other bed, the old man watched one TV show after another. Finally Justin heard him snoring softly.

At last the nurse came in, checked the IV bag, announced, "All right, you're done," and detached the tube. "We'll just leave the needle in for a few days, in case you need it again." Justin looked down at the bandage on the back of his hand. If he'd known that was all there was to it, he'd have been out of the hospital hours ago!

"Now here's something to help with the pain," the nurse was saying. She handed him a glass of water and a tiny paper cup that held two blue pills.

"Thanks," Justin said. He was afraid to take anything that might make him sleep. He put his hand up to his mouth as if he were taking the pills. Then he took a big sip of the water. The nurse checked on the old man and bustled away to the next room.

Justin reached for the remote control next to his bed and shut the TV off. The old man didn't stir. Justin listened to the sounds out in the hallway and in other rooms. Bit by bit, the hospital grew quiet.

He couldn't bear to wait any longer, sitting here as if he had a big target painted on his chest! He slid his legs out from under the sheet, put his feet on the floor, and pushed himself up until he was sitting. Oh, his head hurt! But everything else seemed to be all right. Except for the bandage on his hand where the IV needle was, there didn't seem to be a mark on him from his second meeting with the street.

He stood up. For a moment, his legs felt like water. He had to grab for the end of the bed to keep from falling. He hung on for a long moment until the room stopped spinning around him. How was he going to do this?

He had to do this. He let go of the bed and took a step toward the middle of the room. His knees were shaking—he could actually see them shaking under the short hospital gown. But he kept going.

He passed his own closet and stopped in front of the next one. He glanced toward the hallway, which seemed to be empty. Then he looked back at the old man who seemed to be sleeping soundly. He opened the closet.

Inside, the old man's suit coat and pants were carefully hung on a hanger. Next to them hung a shirt, and on a shelf above was a hat. A pair of shoes sat neatly side by side on the floor of the closet, and a cane leaned in the corner.

Justin grabbed everything, closed the closet door, and shuffled into the bathroom. It took him several minutes to climb into the clothes. Every time he leaned down, the room started to spin again.

The old man's pants were a little short, and the suit coat hung around his stomach with plenty of extra room. The shoes felt strange on his bare feet. He thought about going to his own closet for his socks, but he didn't want to take any more time. Jamming the hat down over his head and grabbing the cane, he opened the bathroom door and peeked out into the room. Everything was quiet.

He took a moment to fluff up his pillow and pull the sheet up over it. It didn't really look as if there were a body in the bed, but it would have to do.

He leaned out the door and looked down the hallway. At the nurse's station he could see the back of someone's head, turned away from him. He stepped out of the room.

Running one hand along the wall to keep himself steady and tapping the cane along the floor with the other, he shuffled toward the elevator at the other end of the hallway. If only his head didn't hurt so much! It was hard to think. He pushed the button for the elevator.

The elevator bell rang once. The elevator door slid open slowly. Inside, two men stepped forward toward him. They both wore white jackets, but their pants were brown and wrinkled. Their shoes were dirty. No matter what they were wearing, Justin would have known them anywhere.

The men stepped out of the elevator. Justin shrank down inside the old man's clothes and tipped his head forward so that the hat covered his face. Leaning heavily on the cane, he stepped into the elevator. He didn't dare turn around to see if they were looking at him. Slowly, slowly, the door slid shut behind him.

He pushed the button for the first floor. Then, as the elevator began to move downward, he thought again and pushed the button for the second floor.

When he got out on the second floor, he found himself in the business office of the hospital. The hallway was empty, and all the rooms were dark. A lighted sign directed him to the stairs. Carefully, he opened the door to the stairwell.

Above him, he heard feet pounding down the stairs toward him. "I can't believe the little rat's given us the slip!" a voice growled. "The last time I checked on him, he was out cold!"

"Well, he can't have got far on foot—and I don't think he'll try a bicycle after that smack on the head! We'll find him!"

Hurriedly Justin pulled the door shut again. He scooted behind the reception desk and crouched down on the floor. It felt so good to rest. He sat down on the floor, then lay down all the way. He'd just rest for a couple of minutes, he told himself. Just for a couple of minutes. That's where the receptionist found him the next morning.

*   *   *

It was lucky for Justin that the receptionist came in early to catch up on some work. She was too frightened to be alone with the strange, rumpled man curled up under her desk. She ran off down the hallway to another department to telephone for the security guard. That gave Justin a moment or two to figure out *who* he was and *where* he was. He figured that he'd have time later to work on remembering *why*.

He dragged himself to his feet, holding himself up by hanging onto the receptionist's desk. His stomach churned. His head was pounding, and he felt stiff all over. He didn't have time to think about that. All he knew was that he had to get out of there.

He spotted the sign for the door to the stairs. He worked his way around the desk and lunged for the door. Made it! By the time he had scuffled down the stairs in the old man's shoes and out into the main lobby of the hospital, he was beginning to feel better.

People arriving for work gave him strange looks as he walked past them in the old man's clothes. He held his head up and walked steadily through the lobby, trying to look as if he dressed this way every day. He had to get out of there before the security guard spotted him. If they put him in a mental ward, he'd *never* get out of here!

There was the front door ahead of him. He listened for running feet or shouting voices, but all was quiet. He pushed open the front door and stepped out onto the street. He was free!

Morning traffic was rushing by—cars and more cars. He felt very alone and exposed out there by himself on the sidewalk. He hurried along the front of the hospital and stepped into the coffee shop next door.

What was he going to do now? He couldn't do this by himself. He had to get some help.

A phone booth stood in the front corner of the coffee shop near the plate glass window. He pushed open the door and stood staring at the phone. Money. He needed money for a phone call.

He pushed his hand into the pocket of the old man's pants. He pulled out a small wad of stuff—bits of paper with numbers written on them in a shaky handwriting, paper clips, and a few coins. Justin picked through the coins until he found a quarter and shoved it into the slot on the phone. He dialed Hugo's number. The phone rang and rang, but there was no answer.

He tried Heather's number. Her answering machine came on. By the number of beeps Justin knew that she had a lot of messages waiting. He hung up. He didn't dare to leave a message on her machine.

What day of the week was it anyway? She must be at work! He found another quarter and dialed the day care center. Mrs. Santos, the director, answered. "Hello, Justin, you're looking for Heather?" she said. "No, she's not here. She asked for yesterday off, but I expected her today. I've called her apartment, but all I got was the answering machine. Is she all right?"

Oh, I hope so! Justin thought. *Oh, Heather, what have I gotten you into?* But all he said was, "Thank you very much, Mrs. Santos. When I speak with her, I'll tell her to call you." He hung up.

He leaned his face against the glass in the phone booth. His stomach was heaving again, and his legs felt weak. His head hurt so much that it was hard to think. He didn't want to think anyway, because all he could think about was Heather. What had happened to her?

He looked out through the window at the street. The black Jaguar was just pulling up in front of the hospital.

CHAPTER 9

Justin's knees turned to water. He sank down inside the phone booth until he was sitting on the floor, out of sight. Now what was he going to do? The phone book was dangling open on a chain in front of his face. *A whole city full of people*, he thought bitterly, *and I can't think of anyone to call.*

Then he looked at it again. At the top of the page in front of his eyes was a name in dark print: GRASSO. He could call Mrs. Grasso! She might know where Heather was!

He searched the phone book page until he found an L. Grasso on Heather's street. Then he pawed through the wad from the old man's pocket. No quarters. A dime, a nickel, another nickel—He reached into the pocket on the other side and pulled out one more nickel.

He knelt on the floor and reached up to put the money in the slot. A woman walking by the phone booth gave him a strange look, but he ignored her. He dialed Mrs. Grasso's number and listened to the rings. He realized he had stopped breathing.

"Hello?" said Mrs. Grasso's cheerful voice.

"Mrs. Grasso, this is Justin Cobb. By any chance, have you seen Heather lately?"

"Justin! Where are you? Heather's been looking all over for you! She's been worried sick!"

"Oh, Mrs. Grasso!" Justin started to jump up, then remembered and stayed down. "Mrs. Grasso, is Heather all right?"

"Yes, she's fine, but where have you been?"

"Um, I've been in the hospital. I'm out now. But I have a problem." He told Mrs. Grasso about the men at the hospital and the black Jaguar. "I'm hiding in a phone booth in the coffee shop next door."

"Well, don't move! I've got a car, you know. I'll be right down to get you. It'll take me about fifteen minutes if the traffic's not too bad."

*　　*　　*

It was a long fifteen minutes, but she came. Justin thought about how they looked as she helped him out of the coffee shop. A fat old lady and a skinny old man shuffling across the sidewalk and getting into a little old black sedan while a little poodle tried to jump all over them.

It felt great to be sitting in Mrs. Grasso's kitchen again, drinking a glass of milk and eating another piece of that cake. It felt even better when Heather and Hugo came through the door. Heather threw herself straight into Justin's arms. "I was sure they'd killed you!" she said. Then she burst into tears.

Justin patted her, hugged her, and finally kissed her all over her wet face, even if Mrs. Grasso and Hugo were watching. "I've been so scared for you and Hugo too," he said. "I didn't know if those guys knew you were with me."

"Naw," Hugo said. "They just ran right past us. But we got out of there fast just in case."

"What about the disk?" Justin asked. "Where is it now?"

Hugo looked embarrassed. "We forgot all about it," Heather explained. "And when we went back to the hotel, that booth was empty. Everything had been taken away."

"You mean they've got the disk? What computer company was it? You were talking to the guy, Hugo! What company was he from?"

Hugo hung his head. "I don't know. I talked to so many of them at the computer fair. I'm sorry." He jammed his hands in his pockets and turned away.

Justin sighed. His head was hurting again, and he wished he could lie down and rest. "I don't know what to do," he said. "Those guys aren't going to give up until they get that disk or me. And I don't even know who they are or what it's all about."

"Hey!" said Hugo. "What's this?" He pulled a card out of his pocket and looked at it. Then he turned toward Justin and grinned. "This might just possibly be what we need!"

"What is it?" Justin asked.

"It's a business card for the Computer Ease Company. That's the one!" Hugo told him. "The guy in the booth gave me the card just before you showed up. I guess I stuck it in my pocket when I found your disk. I forgot all about it in all the running around we've done since then." He held the card up to show it to Justin. "With any luck, the information from the disk is still in that computer."

Justin sank back in his chair and put his hands over his face. "I don't know, Hugo," he said. "You and your pockets!"

* * *

Heather tried to talk Justin into staying at Mrs. Grasso's apartment to rest, but Justin insisted on going with the others to visit the Computer Ease Company. In the end, Mrs. Grasso drove them all across the city in her old sedan. Justin felt somewhat better—but not much—in some of Hugo's clothes.

The salesman looked up and smiled as the four of them entered the store. "What can I do for you folks?" he asked.

Hugo held up the business card. "I was talking to you at the computer fair at the Hanover Hotel," he said. "I was looking at your new Plinex 5000." Behind him, Justin sighed. Good old Hugo couldn't remember the name of the company, but he knew which computer he'd been looking at!

"Ah, yes," the salesman said. "I thought you looked familiar. We have a Plinex 5000 right here, if you'd like to take another look." He pointed to a computer on the counter.

"Well, actually, I was hoping to have a look at the same machine that was on display at the fair. You see, I accidentally left my own disk in it, and—"

"Oh, I'm so sorry," the salesman said. "We did find a disk in our display model when we got it back here to the store. We had no way of knowing whose disk it was, so we threw it away. If we'd known—"

"Where is the display model?" Hugo asked. "Did you clean the programs off it when you brought it back?"

"Oh, I don't think we've had time to do anything to it. I think it's back here in the workshop. Would you like to have a look?"

They would. All four of them crowded after the salesman into the workroom. Heather squeezed Justin's hand as Hugo turned on the computer and started to click through the screens with the mouse.

"Well, I have another customer. Call me if you need me," the salesman said, stepping back into the showroom.

Justin and Heather leaned over Hugo's shoulders. Mrs. Grasso stood on tiptoe and finally pushed between them. "Well?" Justin demanded. "Is the information still on there?"

"Just a minute." Hugo said. "It's got a password, of course, but that's never stopped me before. Let me just try something. Ah! Here it is!"

The computer screen was suddenly full of words and numbers. As Hugo scrolled down the screen, the others could see that the words were names and addresses. And the numbers were amounts of money—large amounts of money.

"What is it?" Justin asked. "What was worth killing someone for?"

Heather was reading the names as they crawled up the screen. "Wait!" she said suddenly. "Hugo, go back! The name just up there! What was it?"

Hugo tapped on the "up" arrow key, and the name came back into view: *Little Friends Day Care Center.*

"That's where I work!" Heather said. "What does it say about it?"

Hugo peered at the rest of the line. "It says *New roof, renovate kitchen. Contract awarded to Peerless Construction Company, 782 North 185th Street. Payment, June 30: $128,000.*" He whistled. "That must be one nice kitchen, Heather. Is your roof gold-plated?"

"But we never got a new kitchen! Or a new roof, either! That roof leaks every time it rains, and the kitchen—Ugh! We applied last spring to the Department of Children's Services, but we never heard from them!"

"I'm not surprised!" Mrs. Grasso called from the other side of the room. She was standing by the salesman's desk with a city telephone book in her hand. "There's no listing for a Peerless Construction Company."

"Come to think of it," Justin said, "we don't deliver out that far by bicycle, but I'm pretty good on the city maps. I'm not so sure there's a North 185th Street."

"What does it say under the entry for the day care center?" Heather said.

Hugo looked at the screen and shook his head. "Here's why you never heard about your application! *Gerald Nelson, Department of Children's Services, $50,000.* A bunch of other people got a chunk of money too."

"Kickbacks! And the city paid for construction projects that were never done! The crooks! Oh, they make me so mad!" growled Mrs. Grasso.

"How are you folks coming?" the salesman asked from the doorway.

"We'll be done in just a second!" Hugo called out. He yanked a disk out of his pocket, slid it into the computer's slot, and clicked quickly on the mouse. The screen changed and went blank. He popped the disk out of the computer and slipped it into his pocket. Then he shut off the computer. "Thanks a million," he said to the salesman as they all walked out to the car.

"Did you get the information?" Justin asked.

"I always carry a blank disk. You never know when it might come in handy," Hugo said, patting his pocket.

"You and your pockets," Justin muttered.

*   *   *

"But what about Albert Worth?" Justin asked as they made their way through the city traffic in Mrs. Grasso's car. "Who killed him and why? And who's the man in the black Jaguar?"

"Maybe Mr. Worth found out about the scheme. Maybe he was going to tell everyone about it. The man in the Jaguar was making a lot of money, so he killed Mr. Worth to stop him from blowing the whistle," Heather said. "He must have known that Mr. Worth was expecting the disk with the proof on it, and he went into Mr. Worth's office and killed him."

"That's a nice idea," Hugo said, "but how about the guy in the business suit, the one who gave Justin the package in the first place? He didn't look like Mr. Nice Guy either. I'm guessing that there was some blackmail going on. When Worth didn't have the package like he'd promised—"

"Well, I think that when the police check this out, they're going to find that the man with the Jaguar also owns a lot of fake construction companies," said Mrs. Grasso. "And I hope he spends a lot of time in jail for stealing our money!" To express her anger, she blasted the horn at a passing taxi, startling everyone in the car including herself.

"So what are you going to do with the disk now, Justin?" Heather asked. "Are you going to go to the police? What if the information on the disk doesn't help them figure out who the killer is? He might still be after you!"

Justin just sat back and leaned his head against the back of the seat. He was much too tired to figure this all out. All he wanted was sleep.

* * *

Mrs. Grasso fixed them all a big pot of spaghetti. She made a special fuss over Justin. She was very glad to see that he was eating well to get his strength back. "It sure beats the hospital's soup!" Justin told her.

When they had all eaten as much as they could hold, Mrs. Grasso cleared away the plates. Then she sat down in her chair and faced the other three. "Okay," she said. "We have to take Justin back to the hospital to get that needle out of his hand." She smiled at Justin's startled look. "Yes, yes, I had surgery a year ago. I know what kind of bandage that is. Imagine just sneaking out of a hospital! What is this world coming to?" Her delighted laugh made it clear that she was proud of Justin for outsmarting the entire hospital. "But first we have to decide what we're going to do with that disk," she said.

Everyone looked at Justin. "Look," Justin said. "We know this disk has got some very hot stuff on it. But we don't know for sure that it will pin whoever killed Mr. Worth or identify the guys who have been chasing me and put them in jail. I'm sick and tired of running and hiding. I'm tired of wearing other people's clothes!"

"But you might get a reward, Justin," said Mrs. Grasso.

"I don't want any reward." Justin sighed. "I just want my old life back. No, that's not quite true. Actually," he said, taking Heather's hand in his, "I was kind of hoping for a new life. A life that includes you."

"Ooh," breathed Mrs. Grasso. "I think he just proposed!" Hugo looked impressed. Even the poodle was wagging its tail.

They all looked at Heather. Her cheeks were wet. "Oh, Justin," she said. "Oh, yes!"

"So what I'd like to do," Justin went on, grinning foolishly, "is to find some way to get the information to the police without anyone knowing where it came from. Is there some way to do that?" he asked Hugo.

"Sure!" Hugo said. "I'll take it over to my apartment and e-mail it from my computer."

"You'll what?" asked Mrs. Grasso.

"I'll send it by electronic mail," he explained. "I don't know the e-mail address for the police, but I can send it to every newspaper in the city." He grinned. "That ought to do it!"

"Sounds good to me," said Justin. "Is that all right with everybody?"

Hugo nodded. "It's your disk! I'm just your computer consultant."

"We just want you to be safe," Heather said. Her eyes were shining.

"And we want the fake construction company guy to go to jail!" Mrs. Grasso growled. Then she smiled. "Okay, if that's settled, let's get Justin back to that hospital for a checkup. Then he can get his own clothes back." She pointed to a bag by the door. "I have your borrowed clothes all ready to go, Justin."

"I owe that poor old guy seventy-five cents," Justin said. "And I think I left his cane somewhere on the second floor, maybe under that desk where I spent the night."

Heather giggled. "Yes, we'd better get Justin back to the hospital. He needs his head examined."

"That's not funny," Justin said, giving her a hug. "Hugo, you can take care of the e-mail?"

"Yes, I'm going to take it to the public library so it can't be traced."

"As soon as you've sent it, get rid of the disk!" Justin told him.

"Don't worry!" Hugo said. "I wouldn't want *my* apartment to be trashed!"

"Who'd notice?" Heather asked.

"I *must* need my head examined, trusting Hugo with the disk again," Justin said.

*   *   *

Over the next few weeks, Justin and Heather and Mrs. Grasso became great fans of the city's newspapers. Day after day, big black headlines told the unfolding story of kickbacks and fraud, construction projects that never happened, construction companies that never existed but got paid anyway. The police made more arrests every day. Almost every department in the city government was touched by the scandal.

It made great reading. It was all that anyone in the city could talk about.

Justin and Heather looked carefully through every article, trying to read between the lines to see if they

could spot the man in the business suit or the owner of
the black Jaguar. One day the newspapers reported that
Albert Worth's murder was thought to have been
carried out by a man named Eric Snyder. Worth may
have demanded extra money from Snyder for setting
up a fake company. Snyder, the newspapers said, was a
local businessman who didn't seem to have any real
business. His only two employees were described as
hired guns.

"Sounds like our friends," Heather said.

"Yes," Justin agreed. "I guess poor Mr. Worth just got
in over his head, playing with the big guys. I think
we're safe."

The next day Heather came home with the news
that the day care center's application had been
approved by the Department of Children's Services.
The new roof would go on next week. "Isn't that great?"
Heather asked. "If we get this building fixed up, this day
care center could be a wonderful place to work!"

"Speaking of working, I've been job hunting," Justin
said. "I've decided not to go back to the bicycle
delivery place. That's no job for a married man!"

"Oh, Justin!" Heather wrapped her arms around his
neck and kissed him.

"Of course, I'm going to get my racing bicycle fixed
up, just for fun."

"Just be careful," Heather said.

"Oh, I'll be all right. I can take care of myself when I
hit the street."

"You've hit it twice. That's enough," Heather said
and kissed him again.